DARE TO LOVE

Carly Phillips

*To all the self-published and indie authors who
paved the way for me to make this leap,*
THANK YOU!

ONE

Once a year, the Dare siblings gathered at the Club Meridian Ballroom in South Florida to celebrate the birthday of the father many of them despised. Ian Dare raised his glass filled with Glenlivet and took a sip, letting the slow burn of fine scotch work its way down his throat and into his system. He'd need another before he fully relaxed.

"Hi, big brother." His sister Olivia strode up to him and nudged him with her elbow.

"Watch the drink," he said, wrapping his free arm around her shoulders for an affectionate hug. "Hi, Olivia."

She returned the gesture with a quick kiss on his cheek. "It's nice of you to be here."

He shrugged. "I'm here for Avery and for you. Although why you two forgave him—"

"Uh-uh. Not here." She wagged a finger in front of his face. "If I have to put on a dress, we're going to act civilized."

Ian stepped back and took in his twenty-four-year-old sister for the first time. Wearing a gold gown, her dark hair up in a chic twist, it was hard to believe she was the same bane of his existence who'd chased after him and his friends until they relented and let her play ball with them.

"You look gorgeous," he said to her.

1

She grinned. "You have to say that."

"I don't. And I mean it. I'll have to beat men off with sticks when they see you." The thought darkened his mood.

"You do and I'll have your housekeeper short-sheet your bed! Again, there should be perks to getting dressed like this, and getting laid should be one of them."

"I'll pretend I didn't hear that," he muttered and took another sip of his drink.

"You not only promised to come tonight, you swore you'd behave."

Ian scowled. "Good behavior ought to be optional considering the way he flaunts his assets," he said with a nod toward where Robert Dare held court.

Around him sat his second wife of nine years, Savannah Dare, and their daughter, Sienna, along with their nearest and dearest country club friends. Missing were their other two sons, but they'd show up soon.

Olivia placed a hand on his shoulder. "He loves her, you know. And Mom's made her peace."

"Mom had no choice once she found out about *her*."

Robert Dare had met the much younger Savannah Sheppard and, to hear him tell it, fallen instantly in love. She was now the mother of his three other children, the oldest of whom was twenty-five. Ian had just turned thirty. Anyone could do the math and come up with two families at the same time. The man was beyond fertile, that was for damned sure.

At the reminder, Ian finished his drink and placed the tumbler on a passing server's tray. "I showed my face. I'm out of here." He started for the exit.

"Ian, hold on," his sister said, frustration in her tone.

"What? Do you want me to wait until they sing 'Happy Birthday'? No thanks. I'm leaving."

Before they could continue the discussion, their half brother Alex strode through the double entrance with a spectacular-looking woman holding tightly to his arm, and Ian's plans changed.

Because of *her*.

Some people had presence; others merely wished they possessed that magic something. In her bold, red dress and fuck-me heels, she owned the room. And he wanted to own her. Petite and curvy, with long, chocolate-brown hair that fell down her back in wild curls, she was the antithesis of every too-thin female he'd dated and kept at arm's length. But she was with his half brother, which meant he had to steer clear.

"I thought you were leaving," Olivia said from beside him.

"I am." He should. If he could tear his gaze away from *her*.

"If you wait for Tyler and Scott, you might just relax enough to have fun," she said of their brothers. "Come on, please?" Olivia used the pleading tone he never could resist.

"Yeah, please, Ian? Come on," his sister Avery said, joining them, looking equally mature in a silver gown that showed way too much cleavage. At twenty-two, she was similar in coloring and looks to Olivia, and he wasn't any more ready to think of her as a grown-up—never mind letting other men ogle her—than he was with her sister.

Ian set his jaw, amazed these two hadn't been the death of him yet.

"So what am I begging him to do?" Avery asked Olivia.

Olivia grinned. "I want him to stay and hang out for a while. Having fun is probably out of the question, but I'm trying to persuade him to let loose."

"Brat," he muttered, unable to hold back a smile at Olivia's persistence.

He stole another glance at his lady in red. He could no more leave than he could approach her, he thought, frustrated because he was a man of action, and right now, he could do nothing but watch her.

"Well?" Olivia asked.

He forced his gaze to his sister and smiled. "Because you two asked so nicely, I'll stay." But his attention remained on the woman now dancing and laughing with his half brother.

* * *

Riley Taylor felt his eyes on her from the moment she entered the elegantly decorated ballroom on the arm of another man. As it was, her heels made it difficult enough to maneuver gracefully. Knowing a devastatingly sexy man watched her every move only made not falling on her ass even more of a challenge.

Alex Dare, her best friend, was oblivious. Being the star quarterback of the Tampa Breakers meant he was used to stares and attention. Riley wasn't. And since this was his father's birthday bash, he knew everyone here. She didn't.

She definitely didn't know *him*. She'd managed to avoid this annual party in the past with a legitimate work excuse one year, the flu another, but this year, Alex knew she was down in the dumps due to job problems, and he'd insisted she come along and have a good time.

While Alex danced with his mother then sisters, she headed for the bar and asked the bartender for a glass of ice water. She took a sip and turned to go find a seat, someplace where she could get off her feet and slip free of her offending heels.

She'd barely taken half a step when she bumped into a hard, suit-clad body. The accompanying jolt sent her water spilling from the top of her glass and into her cleavage. The chill startled her as much as the liquid that dripped down her chest.

"Oh!" She teetered on her stilettos, and big, warm hands grasped her shoulders, steadying her.

She gathered herself and looked up into the face of the man she'd been covertly watching. "You," she said on a breathy whisper.

His eyes, a steely gray with a hint of blue in the depths, sparkled in amusement and something more. "Glad you noticed me too."

She blinked, mortified, no words rushing into her brain to save her. She was too busy taking him in. Dark brown hair stylishly cut, cheekbones perfectly carved, and a strong jaw completed the package. And the most intense heat emanated from his touch as he held on to her arms. His big hands made her feel small, not an easy feat when she was always conscious of her too-full curves.

She breathed in deeply and was treated to a masculine, woodsy scent that turned her insides to pure mush. Full-scale awareness rocked her to her core. This man hit all her right buttons.

"Are you all right?" he asked.

"I'm fine." Or she would be if he'd release her so she could think. Instead of telling him so, she continued to stare into his handsome face.

"You certainly are," he murmured.

A heated flush rushed to her cheeks at the compliment, and a delicious warmth invaded her system.

"I'm sorry about the spill," he said.

At least she hoped he was oblivious to her ridiculous attraction to him.

"You're wet." He released her and reached for a napkin from the bar.

Yes, she was. In wholly inappropriate ways considering they'd barely met. Desire pulsed through her veins. Oh my God, what was it about this man that caused reactions in her body another man would have to work overtime to achieve?

He pressed the thin paper napkin against her chest and neck. He didn't linger, didn't stroke her anywhere he shouldn't, but she could swear she felt the heat of his fingertips against her skin. Between his heady scent and his deliberate touch, her nerves felt raw and exposed. Her breasts swelled, her nipples peaked, and she shivered, her body tightening in places she'd long thought dormant. If he noticed, he was too much of a gentleman to say.

No man had ever awakened her senses this way before. Sometimes she wondered if that was a deliberate choice on her part. Obviously not, she thought and forced herself to step back, away from his potent aura.

He crinkled the napkin and placed the paper onto the bar.

"Thank you," she said.

"My pleasure." The word, laced with sexual innuendo, rolled off his tongue, and his eyes darkened, an indication that this crazy attraction she experienced wasn't one-sided.

"Maybe now we can move on to introductions. I'm Ian Dare," he said.

She swallowed hard, disappointment rushing through her as she realized, for all her awareness of him, he was the one man at this party she ought to stay away from. "Alex's brother."

"Half brother," he bit out.

"Yes." She understood his pointed correction. Alex wouldn't want any more of a connection to Ian than Ian did to Alex.

"You have your father's eyes," she couldn't help but note.

His expression changed, going from warm to cold in an instant. "I hope that's the only thing you think that bastard and I have in common."

Riley raised her eyebrows at the bitter tone. Okay, she understood he had his reasons, but she was a stranger.

Ian shrugged, his broad shoulders rolling beneath his tailored, dark suit. "What can I say? Only a bastard would live two separate lives with two separate families at the same time."

"You do lay it out there," she murmured.

His eyes glittered like silver ice. "It's not like everyone here doesn't know it."

Though she ought to change the subject, he'd been open, so she decided to ask what was on her mind. "If you're still so angry with him, why come for his birthday?"

"Because my sisters asked me to," he said, his tone turning warm and indulgent.

A hint of an easier expression changed his face from hard and unyielding to devastatingly sexy once more.

"Avery and Olivia are much more forgiving than me," he explained.

She smiled at his obvious affection for his siblings. As an only child, she envied them a caring, older brother. At least she'd had Alex, she thought and glanced around looking for the man who'd brought her here. She found him on the dance floor, still with his mother, and relaxed.

"Back to introductions," Ian said. "You know my name; now it's your turn."

"Riley Taylor."

"Alex's girlfriend," he said with disappointment. "I saw you two walk in."

That's what he thought? "No, we're friends. More like brother and sister than anything else."

His eyes lit up, and she caught a glimpse of yet another expression—pleasantly surprised. "That's the best news I've heard all night," he said in a deep, compelling tone, his hot gaze never leaving hers.

At a loss for words, Riley remained silent.

"So, Ms. Riley Taylor, where were you off to in such a hurry?" he asked.

"I wanted to rest my feet," she admitted.

He glanced down at her legs, taking in her red pumps. "Ahh. Well, I have just the place."

Before she could argue—and if she'd realized he'd planned to drag her off alone, she might have—Ian grasped her arm and guided her to the exit at the far side of the room.

"Ian—"

"Shh. You'll thank me later. I promise." He pushed open the door, and they stepped out onto a deck that wasn't in use this evening.

Sticky, night air surrounded them, but being a Floridian, she was used to it, and obviously so was he. His arm still cupping her elbow, he led her to a small love seat and gestured for her to sit.

She sensed he was a man who often got his way, and though she'd never found that trait attractive before, on him, it worked. She settled into the soft cushions. He did the same, leaving no space between them, and she liked the feel of his hard body aligned with hers. Her heart beat hard in her chest, excitement and arousal pounding away inside her.

Around them, it was dark, the only light coming from sconces on the nearby building.

"Put your feet up." He pointed to the table in front of them.

"Bossy," she murmured.

Ian grinned. He was and was damned proud of it. "You're the one who said your feet hurt," he reminded her.

"True." She shot him a sheepish look that was nothing short of adorable.

The reverberation in her throat went straight to Ian's cock, and he shifted in his seat, pure sexual desire now pumping through his veins.

He'd been pissed off and bored at his father's ridiculous birthday gala. Even his sisters had barely been able to coax a smile from him. Then *she'd* walked into the room.

Because she was with his half brother, Ian hadn't planned on approaching her, but the minute he'd caught sight of her alone at the bar, he'd gone after her, compelled by a force beyond his understanding. Finding out she and Alex were just friends had made his night because she'd provide a perfect distraction to the pain that followed him whenever his father's other family was near.

"Shoes?" he reminded her.

She dipped her head and slipped off her heels, moaning in obvious relief.

"That sound makes me think of other things," he said, capturing her gaze.

"Such as?" She unconsciously swayed closer, and he suppressed a grin.

"Sex. With you."

"Oh." Her lips parted with the word, and Ian couldn't tear his gaze away from her lush, red-painted mouth.

A mouth he could envision many uses for, none of them tame.

"Is this how you charm all your women?" she asked. "Because I'm not sure it's working." A teasing smile lifted her lips, contradicting her words.

He had her, all right, as much as she had him.

He kept his gaze on her face, but he wasn't a complete gentleman and couldn't resist brushing his hand over her tight nipples showing through the fabric of her dress.

Her eyes widened in surprise at the same time a soft moan escaped, sealing her fate. He slid one arm across the love seat until his fingers hit her mass of curls, and he wrapped his hand in the thick strands. Then, tugging her close, he sealed his mouth over hers. She opened for him immediately. The first taste was a mere preview, not nearly enough, and he deepened the kiss, taking more.

Sweet, hot, and her tongue tangled with his. He gripped her hair harder, wanting still more. She was like all his favorite vices in one delectable package. Best of all, she kissed him back, every inch a willing, giving partner.

He was a man who dominated and took, but from the minute he tasted her, he gave as well. If his brain were clear, he'd have pulled back immediately, but she reached out and gripped his shoulders, curling her fingers through the fabric of his shirt, her nails digging into his skin. Each thrust of his tongue in her mouth mimicked what he really wanted, and his cock hardened even more.

"You've got to be kidding me," his half brother said, interrupting at the worst possible moment.

He would have taken his time, but Riley jumped, pushing at his chest and backing away from him at the same time.

"Alex!"

"Yeah. The guy who brought you here, remember?"

Ian cursed his brother's interruption as much as he welcomed the reminder that this woman represented everything Ian resented. His half brother's friend. Alex, with whom he had a rivalry that would have done real siblings proud.

The oldest sibling in the *other* family was everything Ian wasn't. Brash, loud, tattoos on his forearms, and he threw a mean football as quarterback of the Tampa Breakers. Ian, meanwhile, was more of a thinker, president of the Breakers' rivals, the Miami Thunder, owned by his father's estranged brother, Ian's uncle.

Riley jumped up, smoothing her dress and rubbing at her swollen lips, doing nothing to ease the tension emanating from her best friend.

Ian took his time standing.

"I see you met my brother," Alex said, his tone tight.

Riley swallowed hard. "We were just—"

"Getting better acquainted," Ian said in a seductive tone meant to taunt Alex and imply just how much better he now knew Riley.

A muscle ticked in the other man's jaw. "Ready to go back inside?" Alex asked her.

Neither one of them would make a scene at this mockery of a family event.

"Yes." She didn't meet Ian's gaze as she walked around him and came up alongside Alex.

"Good because my dad's been asking for you. He said it's been too long since he's seen you," Alex said, taunting Ian back with the mention of the one person sure to piss him off.

Despite knowing better, Ian took the bait. "Go on. We were finished anyway," he said, dismissing Riley as surely as she'd done to him.

Never mind that she was obviously torn between her friend and whatever had just happened between them; she'd chosen Alex. A choice Ian had been through before and come out on the same wrong end.

In what appeared to be a deliberately possessive move, Alex wrapped an arm around her waist and led her back inside. Ian watched, ignoring the twisting pain in his gut at the sight. Which was ridiculous. He didn't have any emotional investment in Riley Taylor. He didn't do emotion, period. He viewed relationships through the lens of his father's adultery, finding it easier to remain on the outside looking in.

Distance was his friend. Sex worked for him. It was love and commitment he distrusted. So no matter how different that brief moment with Riley had been, that was all it was.

A moment.

One that would never happen again.

*   *   *

Riley followed Alex onto the dance floor in silence. They hadn't spoken a word to each other since she'd let him lead her away from Ian. She understood his shocked reaction and wanted to soothe his frazzled nerves but didn't know how. Not when her own nerves were so raw from one simple kiss.

Except nothing about Ian was simple, and that kiss left her reeling. From the minute his lips touched hers, everything else around her had ceased to matter. The tug of arousal hit her in the pit of her stomach, in her scalp as his fingers tugged her hair, in the weight of her breasts, between her thighs and, most telling, in her mind. He was a strong man, the kind who knew what he wanted and who liked to get his way. The type of man she usually avoided and for good reason.

But she'd never experienced chemistry so strong before. His pull was so compelling she'd willingly followed him outside regardless of the fact that she knew without a doubt her closest friend in the world would be hurt if she got close to Ian.

"Are you going to talk to me?" Alex asked, breaking into her thoughts.

"I'm not sure what to say."

On the one hand, he didn't have a say in her personal life. She didn't owe him an apology. On the other, he was her everything. The child she'd grown up next door to and the best friend who'd saved her sanity and given her a safe haven from her abusive father.

She was wrong. She knew exactly what to say. "I'm sorry."

He touched his forehead to hers. "I don't know what came over me. I found you two kissing, and I saw red."

"It was just chemistry." She let out a shaky laugh, knowing that term was too benign for what had passed between her and Ian.

"I don't want you to get hurt. The man doesn't do relationships, Ri. He uses women and moves on."

"Umm, Pot/Kettle?" she asked him. Alex moved from woman to woman just as he'd accused his half brother of doing.

He'd even kissed *her* once. Horn dog that he was, he said he'd had to try, but they both agreed there was no spark and their friendship meant way too much to throw away for a quick tumble between the sheets.

Alex frowned. "Maybe so, but that doesn't change the facts about him. I don't want you to get hurt."

"I won't," she assured him, even as her heart picked up speed when she caught sight of Ian watching them from across the room.

Drink in hand, brooding expression on his face, his stare never wavered.

She curled her hands into the suit fabric covering Alex's shoulders and assured herself she was telling the truth.

"What if he was using you to get to me?"

"Because the man can't be interested in me for me?" she asked, her pride wounded despite the fact that Alex was just trying to protect her.

Alex slowed his steps and leaned back to look into her eyes. "That's not what I meant, and you know it. Any man would be lucky to have you, and I'd never get between you and the right guy." A muscle pulsed in Alex's right temple, a sure sign of tension and stress. "But Ian's not that guy."

She swallowed hard, hating that he just might be right. Riley wasn't into one-night stands. Which was why her body's combustible reaction to Ian Dare confused and confounded her. How far would she have let him go if Alex hadn't interrupted? Much further than she'd like to imagine, and her body responded with a full out shiver at the thought.

"Now can we forget about him?"

Not likely, she thought, when his gaze burned hotter than his kiss. Somehow she managed to swallow over the lump in her throat and give Alex the answer he sought. "Sure."

Pleased, Alex pulled her back into his arms to continue their slow dance. Around them, other guests, mostly his father's age, moved slowly in time to the music.

"Did I mention how much I appreciate you coming here with me?" Obviously trying to ease the tension between them, he shot her the same charming grin that had women thinking they were special.

Riley knew better. She *was* special to him, and if he ever turned his brand of protectiveness on the right kind of woman and not the groupies he preferred, he might find himself settled and happy one day. Sadly, he didn't seem to be on that path.

She decided to let their disagreement over Ian go. "I believe you've mentioned how wonderful I am a couple of times. But you still owe me one," Riley said. Parties like this weren't her thing.

"It took your mind off your job stress, right?" he asked.

She nodded. "Yes, and let's not even talk about that right now." Monday was soon enough to deal with her new boss.

"You got it. Ready for a break?" he asked.

She nodded. Unable to help herself, she glanced over where she'd seen Ian earlier, but he was gone. The disappointment twisting the pit of her stomach was disproportional to the amount of time she'd known him, and she blamed that kiss.

Her lips still tingled, and if she closed her eyes and ran her tongue over them, she could taste his heady, masculine flavor. Somehow she had to shake him from her thoughts. Alex's reaction to seeing them together meant Riley couldn't allow herself the luxury of indulging in anything more with Ian.

Not even in her thoughts or dreams.

TWO

Riley walked into the main office of Blunt Sporting Goods, a manufacturer and retailer where she'd been employed since she was seventeen. She'd worked her way up from sales to store manager until she was ultimately drafted into their corporate headquarters after college. She worked hard, earned good money, and best of all, loved her job. She was in charge of distribution and knew how to get their goods into the right hands. Too bad all those years of loyal service were now threatened by a sale to new owners.

When Jerry Blunt had decided to retire and travel with his wife, he'd sold the once-family-owned business to a pompous jerk who'd withheld his intentions of cleaning house and bringing in fresh new talent, as he called his hires, until the final papers were signed.

He brought in all his own people for lead jobs, which Riley grudgingly admitted made sense. But he also sought to hire new people from outside the company, those willing to work for less money. He didn't give the long-standing, once-valued workers a chance to prove their worth. Many older employees with families to support were let go and they'd have a tough time getting a new job for the same pay.

It sucked, Riley thought, and she wanted to at least try and save her department. To do so, she had to prove to her new boss that she could run things well and efficiently and make him money. Sadly, he wasn't the type to listen, and every day, more people left with their belongings in a box, escorted out by security.

When her intercom rang, calling her in to see the new boss, Riley had no doubt she would be the next one out the door. She flexed her fingers and rose, taking the stairs to the next floor, using the time to give herself a pep talk before approaching Franklin O'Mara.

"Go on in," Gail, his personal secretary, also new to the company, said. "He's expecting you."

"Thanks." She stepped into his office.

In his forties with a receding hairline and paunch in his stomach, he epitomized the lazy executive, and it killed Riley to see the company she loved be destroyed by someone who didn't see the value of the employees he'd inherited.

"Ms. Taylor." He held a file in his hand, no doubt filled with her evaluations and track record at the company.

"Mr. O'Mara." She waited until he gestured for her to be seated before nodding and settling into the chair across from his massive desk.

"I'm sorry to say, we'll be letting you go."

She swallowed hard. "I understand your new corporate policy involves bringing in fresh talent," she began.

"Then you understand it's nothing personal. We'll give you a good severance package and references. Marge in HR will discuss the details with you."

"What if I told you I could get you access to the Miami Thunder?" she asked, grasping at the first—and clearly most absurd—thing that came to mind.

No doubt because Ian Dare, president of the Miami Thunder, who kissed like a dream, had been in her dreams day and night since their hookup Saturday night.

O'Mara's eyes lit up with interest. "Keep talking."

She ran her tongue along the inside of her dry mouth, wishing she could take back her words. For one thing, Alex would kill her. For another, she didn't even have access to the man.

But she had a department of employees whose jobs and welfare depended on this one Hail Mary. "I have a personal connection with Ian Dare." The lip-lock they'd shared was very personal, she thought, suppressing a shiver.

"Go on."

She crossed her fingers in her lap and continued. "I've been planning on talking to him about changing suppliers for his team's inventory, or at least giving us a shot. I figured once he sees we're reliable and our deals are solid, maybe he'll throw more business our way."

She twisted her fingers, hoping he didn't notice how badly she was panicking as she spoke. Even she knew football teams had major multi-year contracts with big companies, but the words were out, and there was no taking them back.

"Now that's a way to put yourself on my radar." He nodded approvingly. "Okay, talk to him. You have until Friday noon. No deal? I'm bringing in my people."

Riley rose to her feet. "Thank you," she said, extending her hand for his sweaty handshake, then turned and headed for the door.

"Noon Friday," he reminded her as she let herself out.

For the return trip to her office, Riley took the elevator, unsure her legs would support her on the walk down. She didn't want to lose her job, but unless she could reach Ian Dare and talk him into doing business with her, she'd be unemployed, unable to afford her rent, car payment, student loans, and other assorted bills. Even Alex would understand how her utter panic over the possibility had led her to Ian.

She hoped.

She leaned against the elevator wall and groaned. Thanks to her bluster and big mouth, her job was in Ian Dare's very sexy hands.

*   *   *

For the week following his father's party, Ian was tied up in preparation for the football draft. Agents trying to pitch their best players, to trade their unhappy players, to work the system and his team to their advantage. This year, the annual event was being held in Ian's hometown of Miami, at his father's flagship hotel, which meant he'd have to be on guard while he was there. Dealing with Robert Dare's attempts at reconciliation could only distract him from business.

He was so inundated meeting with his general manager and scouts, he only returned calls relating to deals, ignoring all others, including his mother and siblings.

When he finally sat down to eat and listen to all his messages, he was shocked to hear the sexy voice he dreamed about at night.

"Hi, Ian. It's Riley Taylor. We—umm—met at your father's birthday party this past weekend. I have something important I'd like to discuss with you. My number is…" He listened to the rest of the message, absently jotting down her information while focusing on her voice.

Strong and husky, her tone aroused him all over again, but he also noticed a tremor as she spoke, which made him wonder if the memory of their kiss haunted her as much as it did him. Since Saturday night, he'd alternated between cursing his half brother for interrupting and being grateful for the reminder that this woman had loyalties in direct conflict with him.

As an adult, Ian hated the notion of considering Alex competition, but the past couldn't be changed. When their father had had a choice to make, he'd picked Alex and his siblings, not Ian and his. They'd had him for concerts, sporting events, and graduations. Maybe not all his father's so-called hotel travel had been a lie, but there was no doubt who'd gotten short shrift when it came to having a dad. And though Ian had stepped up for his siblings, nothing could replace the gaping hole Robert Dare had left them with, both when they were ignorant of the other family and after he'd moved out.

So yes, Alex had always been a rival. First for their father's affection, then as the star quarterback of the Thunder's biggest competition, and now for a woman Ian barely knew. Even if that kiss had made him think they had a connection, her withdrawal afterward had made a bigger statement. This woman had gotten to him, something no other could claim. He wouldn't be giving her another opening. He might be curious as to what she wanted and why she'd reach out to him, but he couldn't afford to care.

He allowed himself a few last lingering thoughts of Riley, the fruity taste of her glossed lips and the sound of her soft moans reverberating through him. Then he picked up the paper on which he'd written down her number, crushed it into a ball, and tossed it in the trash.

*   *   *

For the first two days of the draft, Ian managed to miss bumping into his old man but knew his luck wouldn't hold out. Sure enough, Saturday morning, Robert intercepted him on his way to a breakfast meeting at the restaurant.

"Ian!" His father strode up to him, dressed in a suit and tie, happy as if he owned the world.

Ian inclined his head. "Good morning. I can't talk. I'm late for a meeting."

His father stared at him with knowing eyes. Eyes the same gray as his own. "I won't keep you. But I was disappointed I didn't get to talk to you at the party the other night."

"I was there. Only because Avery and Olivia asked me to come," he deliberately added.

Avery, his youngest sister, had been a bone marrow donor for their father's other daughter, Sienna—Sienna's illness being the only reason Robert Dare had revealed his cheating, lying ways. He'd needed to see if any of his legitimate children were matches. The girls had bonded over the experience, accepting them as family. Ian didn't feel the same way. He didn't hate his half siblings, he just wanted nothing to do with them. But unlike his father, he'd sworn to be there for his family, so when the girls had asked him to attend the party for them, he'd agreed.

"And I'm grateful you attended. A man never knows how many years he has left," Robert said.

Ian rolled his eyes at the dramatic statement. "You're healthy, and you'll probably outlive us all." He deliberately glanced at his watch. "I've got to get inside." He tipped his head toward the restaurant.

"Maybe we can have lunch or dinner?" the older man asked, hope in his eyes.

Ian shook his head. "Like I said, I've got meetings."

Shadows crossed his father's face, and Ian did his best not to feel guilty.

"Fine, but I'll keep trying, you know."

Ian straightened his shoulders. "It's too late for that too." He turned away and stepped toward the restaurant entrance when he heard his name being called and turned.

This time it was Alex rushing to catch up to him.

His father hadn't left, and he greeted his other son, not bothering to excuse himself as Alex strode up to Ian.

"You're such a selfish prick," Alex said, getting into his face. "Would it have killed you to return her phone calls and see what she had to say?"

Ian immediately knew he was talking about Riley. "You're the one who made it clear she should have nothing to do with me, so what's up your ass now?"

"She left you a message, right? Said she had something important to discuss? And you couldn't be bothered to call?" Alex asked, jaw held tight.

In that instant, Ian saw shades of his father in Alex's younger face. It had been awhile since the blood connection between them had hit him so strongly. And damn but it hurt.

"Would one of you tell me what the hell is going on?" Robert asked, interrupting them.

Alex straightened his shoulders. "Riley called him this week. She needed a favor and asked him to call her back. He didn't."

"I was busy," Ian said, suddenly feeling a combination of guilt and overriding concern. "It's draft week, not that I owe you an explanation. Besides, *you* made it clear I should back off." Ian wasn't above sharing the blame when warranted.

Alex ran a hand through his hair, frustration evident in the bulging muscles in his neck. "She's my best friend. Has been since we were kids."

"What did she need from me?" Ian asked, ignoring any reference to how close Riley and Alex were. Even if it was friendship, it had come between Ian and the woman he wanted. He found it difficult to contain his jealousy.

Alex paused, looking torn, before he said, "It's not my story to tell, and besides, it's too late anyway."

"What the hell does that mean?" Ian asked.

"Is Riley okay?" Robert demanded. "I care about that girl like a daughter."

"As if you don't have enough of those," Ian muttered.

His father's face blanched, his skin color leaching out. "She practically lived in our house growing up. If something's wrong, I want to know."

"You know Riley. She's always okay or pretends to be," Alex said. "She's independent and proud and you know it. You also know why. It took enough for her to call *him*." Alex jerked a finger at Ian.

"But if one of us can help—" Robert said, only to be cut off by the abrupt swinging of Alex's hand.

"Let her handle her own shit. I've learned it's the only way to keep her in my life."

Alex turned back to Ian. "I came here because I was furious, and you deserved to know you fucked up. But it's too late now. There's nothing anyone can do."

There were so many questions raised by Alex's statement Ian didn't know where to begin. From her always pretending to be okay, to her being proud and independent, Alex and their father were privy to why. Ian wasn't.

But he wanted to know. Needed to understand her even if it meant digging deeper than she'd be comfortable with. He was also smart enough not to ask questions his half brother wouldn't answer.

"Give me her number," Ian said. "The least I can do is apologize."

Alex scowled at him. "Go to hell. She doesn't need your help anymore. And she sure as hell doesn't need to be another one of your conquests."

"Hey." Ian grabbed his shoulder.

Alex shrugged him away. "Back off."

"Just give me her damned number."

"Not happening, and don't think you can look her up in the phone book. She's unlisted."

With that, he stormed off, leaving Ian where he'd started, about to walk away from his father.

Before he could take leave, his father placed a hand on Ian's shoulder, surprising him and causing an old memory to surface. Robert, getting ready to leave for a business trip, wearing a suit, and placing his hand on ten-year-old Ian's shoulder. "Take care of your mother and siblings, son."

At the time, Ian had been puffed up and proud his father trusted him with the job. Looking back, the request was as much of an illusion as his childhood had been. No ten-year-old could possibly take on that responsibility. It was just something a parent said to make his kid feel important. But the reality was, that had been Ian's job for way too long.

He stood stiffly, refusing to give his father the satisfaction of shoving him away, and waited for him to finish.

"You all don't have to pay for my sins, son. You could get to know each other. You could be brothers."

His suit jacket suddenly too tight, Ian broke into an uncomfortable sweat. "What part of that conversation indicated either of us wants that?"

"You're both men with huge egos. Neither of you is willing to bend first. But you're the oldest. Maybe you won't give me a second chance, but you should give your other siblings a first one. You're all family."

Though he hated giving his father a glimpse into his feelings, Ian raised a hand to his throbbing temple. "Isn't it enough I take care of my brothers, sisters, and mother after you couldn't be bothered? I'm there for them."

"If you ever need me…" His father trailed off as Ian turned to go.

Suddenly, he realized his father had something Ian wanted…or if he didn't have it, he had access. He turned back to the older man. "You can do something for me."

"What is it?" Robert asked, hope in his voice.

"I need to get in touch with Riley. Phone number, address, something. Can you get me that?"

Disappointment flooded Robert's face before he schooled his expression. "I'll give you her number if you do something for me in return."

The calculating son of a bitch, Ian thought. "What is it?" he bit out.

"Reach out to Sienna and the boys. Invite them to lunch or dinner." Robert eyed him speculatively, clearly eager to see what he'd do.

Ian gritted his teeth and didn't answer.

"I thought apologizing to Riley was important to you."

"It is."

His father's deal begged the question, did Ian want access to Riley Taylor badly enough to extend an olive branch to his father's other family?

Her scent came back to him vividly, a fruity blend that had knocked him on his ass and had him daydreaming of her ever since. The thought of putting any kind of pain in those blue eyes was like slicing his own skin, yet apparently he'd done just that. He needed to fix it. But first he needed to know what the hell he'd done by not returning her call.

Hell yes, she was worth it.

Ian forced out the words. "I'll invite Sienna for lunch."

Robert's narrowed gaze settled on Ian. "That's a start."

If Ian had wondered where he got his business sense, he now knew. "I'll include Alex and Jason too," he muttered.

Robert nodded, clearly pleased. "Good. Savannah has Riley's information in her phone," he said of his current wife and Sienna, Alex, and Jason's mother. "I'll send it over to you later today."

"Fine." Ian wasn't about to thank the man for something he'd bribed him for.

Looks like he had a family reunion to plan. Because Riley Taylor had gotten to him that much.

THREE

Riley pulled up to the gate surrounding Alex's mansion on Star Island and entered the key code, letting herself in and driving down his long driveway. Alex's house was a far cry from the small apartment in Miami where Riley lived, but she was used to her best friend's wealth. He had his main house here and a luxury apartment in Tampa for during the season. He needed his privacy, and thanks to the one road in and out along with the guardhouse at the entrance, Alex was away from the prying eyes of rabid fans.

She parked in a guest spot on his driveway, and a few minutes later, she and Alex sat on the floor in his man cave, as he called it, eating pizza he'd had delivered.

"You're really a good friend, letting me cry on your shoulder like this."

He shot her one of his patented, *are you an idiot* looks. "Like you'd do anything different for me?"

She stretched her legs out in front of her, leaning her head back on the couch behind her. "I just can't believe it. I worked so hard for so long. And everything came down to one long shot."

She grabbed a soda instead of a beer, knowing she had to drive home later.

"You'll find something. You're talented, and you've got a kick-ass resume," Alex said in an attempt to reassure her.

She smiled at his unwavering support. "I'll give myself a short window to wallow in self-pity, and then I'm picking myself up and moving on."

"I wouldn't expect anything less from you. When things get rough, you never give in."

"Nope." Because if she had, she'd have become like her mother, and the one thing Riley had promised herself was, she would never be any man's doormat.

"I could make a few calls. Get your foot in the door at—"

"No. Thank you, but no. I can find something on my own."

Alex frowned. "Yet you had no problem calling *him*."

She raised her shoulders, unable to explain why she'd used Ian's name to try and save her job, even to herself.

"Never mind. You were desperate. I get it." Alex repeated what he'd said the first time she told him what she'd done. She'd been so upset with herself, and she'd felt worse when he hadn't even gotten angry. He'd merely pulled her into a hug.

When Alex was being rational, his jealousy and bitterness over how Ian treated him didn't come into play. She'd always sensed Alex would be more open to Ian and his brothers if Ian would do the same.

Alex took a long pull of beer. "The least he could have done was return your call."

"Well, maybe it's for the best. You know how much I hate asking for help. This way, I don't owe him anything."

An annoyed sound rumbled from deep in Alex's chest. "Yes, your best friend who makes millions knows how much you hate asking, taking, or even accepting help."

She shrugged, knowing how much she frustrated him, living in her one-bedroom apartment without a doorman. He considered her like one of his sisters and wanted her to move to a better neighborhood, but she was happy in her space and wanted to live on her own salary. She'd always felt the need to prove she could stand on her own, was worthy on her own merits, no matter what her father used to say.

"You're a pain in the ass," he said.

"At least you know I love you for yourself."

"Amen to that, sweetheart." He tipped his bottle her way. "I still can't believe the SOB didn't call you back," Alex said, returning to the subject of Ian. "It's not like *I* left the damn message," he muttered.

Remembering that kiss and the electricity that had practically crackled in the air around them, she was surprised too. Hadn't Ian been at least curious about what she'd wanted? If she weren't so upset about her career and her future, her feminine ego might be hurt.

"I nearly kicked his ass today," Alex said.

Riley choked on her soda. "You did what? Where did you see him?" She sat up straighter.

"I headed over to the draft hotel. I figured he needed to know what a selfish asshole he is."

"Alex," she groaned. She closed her eyes and leaned back against the sofa. "Couldn't you have left it alone?" Embarrassment already filled her at the thought of Ian's ignoring her call, let alone Alex confronting him over it.

"No, I could not. He needed to be taken down a peg. But don't worry. Dad was there, so we didn't get violent."

She glared at him from across the table.

"And I didn't tell him you lost your job either."

She exhaled long and hard. "Well, at least you spared me that."

He grinned. "Did I mention some of my teammates are coming by for poker tonight? You up to staying? You know the guys enjoy your company."

She groaned. "No thanks." She made a face. She wasn't in the mood for the guys or their crude humor.

He rose to his feet, collecting the pizza box. She stood and grabbed the empties. They cleaned up with an ease born of years of friendship. "Appreciate you being here for me," she said again.

"Always, Ri." He reached out to ruffle her hair, but, expecting the move, she ducked before he could reach her.

By the time she arrived home, she was exhausted. It didn't help that during the drive home, she'd mentally mapped out her future options, which mostly consisted of sending resumes to the big sports and distribution chains, some out of state. The thought of having to start over, prove her worth, and work her way back up the corporate ladder once more made her sick.

She loved Miami and didn't want to leave her stepmother or Alex and her other friends. There were other smaller local companies she planned to scope out, so all wasn't lost yet. And until all was lost, she wouldn't mention it to Alex. He'd only get upset and insist on helping. Obviously, people would bend over backwards to help the superstar, and his best friend by extension, but Riley really wanted to try and find a job on her own first.

She let herself into her building, walked up one flight to her apartment, and was startled to find someone waiting outside her door. Even in the dimly lit hall, she recognized Ian

Dare's tall frame, dark hair, and handsome features. Excitement bubbled up inside her, followed by wariness.

"Finally," he said, leading her to believe he'd been standing there awhile.

She fought against her rapidly beating heart. "What are you doing here?"

He pushed off the wall and strode toward her. "Do you realize I walked into the building without being buzzed in? I just followed behind a couple who were too busy groping each other to pay attention to who was entering behind them."

He didn't have to further sum up his point. Riley already knew the argument well from Alex and her stepmom. "It's perfectly safe. I carry mace and I'm careful. And you still haven't answered my question."

Ian ran a hand through his hair, taking the time to tamp down on the anger that had been brewing inside him as he waited for her in this tiny hall that, despite her claim, was far from safe.

Not for a woman with her full breasts and curvy hips. Not for a woman with that mass of untamed hair and wild beauty, dressed in a short denim skirt with a ruffled edge and black sleeveless top that bared a hint of her stomach.

He fought for control over his libido and the desire to take her in every way imaginable. "I realize I didn't return your call, but I'm here now."

She met his gaze, brave and unwavering. "Go home. Whatever I needed from you, it's too late now."

His eyes narrowed. "That's what Alex said, but he refused to elaborate. He said it was your business, so I came to the source. I was busy this week. I had meetings for the draft, and I couldn't call you back."

She raised an eyebrow. "Bull. I'm guessing there are a whole host of reasons why you didn't get back to me. At the top of the list is that you hate Alex."

"I don't hate him." He clenched his hands and released them again, searching for focus. "Riley, you left me a message. Just tell me why."

"It's too late." She walked toward him as she spoke.

She passed him by, heading for her door, key in hand. "I already lost my job," she said as she slipped inside her apartment.

The door slammed closed behind her, leaving him basking in her scent.

"Son of a bitch." He knocked hard.

When she didn't answer, he tried again.

And again.

Worst-case scenario, he'd settle into the hallway for the night and wait to catch her when she left again in the morning. Unwilling to do that, he banged on the door again.

In the middle of his knock, she swung the door open wide.

"Fine. Come in," she said, her eyes narrowed and wary.

He stepped inside. Once enclosed in her small apartment, her luscious scent wrapped around him once more. His cock took a definite hit as desire filled him along with that burning need only she inspired. Knowing those feelings wouldn't be welcome, he took in her space. Bright colors on the walls, eclectic pieces of furniture, and a warm feel. She knew how to take a tiny area and make it feel like a true home.

"Can I get you something to drink?" she asked.

"No. I just want to know what happened."

She expelled a deep breath, causing her breasts to rise and fall beneath the flimsy material. He glanced down, trying not to ogle her cleavage because that made him want to test the weight of her breasts. And once he started touching her, he wouldn't be able to stop. Instead, he noticed her toenails were painted a bright orange, one toe surrounded by a thin silver ring. Even her fucking feet were sexy.

"I worked for Blunt Sporting Goods," she said, unaware of his train of thought. "I was head of their distribution and sales department. The company was sold; the new boss is an ass and began laying people off. I pulled a Hail Mary and told him I had an in with you, that I could get some of our products distributed to the team. He gave me until Friday to get back to him with something substantial. I called. You didn't. End of story." She strode over to the door and swung it open, obviously eager to get rid of him.

He stared in stunned surprise. "You told him that after meeting me for the first time on Saturday night?"

She raised her chin. "Yep."

"After our kiss."

Her cheeks turned a healthy pink. "Mmm-hmm."

"After you walked away from me without a second glance."

She blinked up at him. "I looked back," she said softly.

He narrowed his gaze. "You've got nerve."

"So I've been told." She grinned.

He smiled back.

She obviously realized they were sharing a moment and turned off the megawatt grin. "So now you know. You can go now." She tilted her chin toward the hallway.

Pride. She had it in spades and didn't like him knowing she'd lost her job. He respected that. Too bad he wasn't about to leave her now.

He shook his head, silently telling her he was staying. The guilt he'd felt when his brother told him he'd caused Riley problems was only magnified now that he knew how. Based on how angry Alex had been on her behalf, he cared about her deeply. He looked after her. And that was something else Ian could respect. Friendship with his half brother, Ian could work around.

But first, there was the issue of her job.

"I realize you don't know me, but you're going to. Because you brought me into your world by calling me, I caused a problem for you. Now I'm obligated to fix it."

She leaned against the still-open door. "You can't, because we both know you're committed to whoever you already purchase from, and I shouldn't have opened my big mouth."

So she'd realized the way of things in the business. Although that ought to alleviate his guilt over her losing her job, it didn't. "Maybe not, but if I'd returned your call, there are other people I could have referred you to who could have given your company business."

"We'll never know, now will we?"

"About that? No." Pretending to be tough and unconcerned didn't fool him for a second.

She lived in this building, in a not-great part of town, because it was all she could afford. With Ian's background in owning investment property, he could figure out her approximate income and rent and knew, though she might have a small savings, she couldn't afford to be unemployed for an extended period of time. So she'd panicked and called him, which meant he owed her.

But that wasn't why he was still here. He wanted to help. She might not let his brother do it, but Ian damned well intended to.

"What are your plans now?" he asked.

She slowly shut the door, obviously realizing he had no intention of leaving. "I'll send out resumes like any job-seeking person would," she said, as if he were dense not to have figured her next step out for himself.

"Or you could come work for me."

The color drained from her face. "You're offering me a job. With the Thunder."

He nodded.

"Doing...?"

If she was questioning, she wasn't saying no, and his heart rate sped up at the possibility of seeing her day in and day out. "That remains to be seen. I know we have some openings. We'll see what fits best."

She swallowed hard and remained silent, but the color had returned to her cheeks. "So I wouldn't be working directly for you."

Interesting the thought of working with him flustered her. Good, because that meant she wasn't immune, no matter how high a wall she'd erected between them.

"No, you won't be working for me. I can't have that."

She wrinkled her nose, making him want to reach out and stroke her soft skin.

"Why not?" she asked.

He stepped closer, and when she didn't back away, closer still, until mere inches separated them. "Because I intend to get to know you personally, Riley Taylor. So I can't be mixing business with pleasure."

Her breath caught, but she remained in place, those huge blue eyes watching him with a mix of wary curiosity and definite desire. He wanted to kiss her again, to lose himself in that luscious mouth, then press her against the wall and thrust into her warm, wet body.

Shit.

He tore his gaze from hers, reminding himself to slow the fuck down. He hadn't gotten her to agree to take a position with the team. A job was her priority, and that meant it was his as well.

Using all the willpower he had, he straightened his shoulders and stepped away first. "Come to the stadium tomorrow morning and ask for Olivia Dare. My sister will find the appropriate fit for you with the organization."

"I can't take charity." She folded her arms across her chest. In her defensive stance, he saw the secrets that Alex knew.

The ones that held the key to understanding this complicated woman. Before he was finished, he intended to know her inside and out.

He remained apart, giving her space. "It's not charity when I owe you for not returning your call. It's not nepotism, favoritism, or any other ism you might come up with either."

She pursed her lips, obviously wavering.

His gaze lingered on her mouth, the desire to take it overwhelming, but he refrained. "You were willing to call me and ask me to do business with you. Consider this a similar opportunity. If you can't do the job, you're out on your ass, the same as anyone else." He gave her the honest truth. He wouldn't keep her on the payroll if she couldn't perform.

"So? What will it be?"

In the ensuing silence, all the possible things Ian wanted to do to her, with her, passed in front of his eyes until he was convinced she'd say no.

"I'll be there in the morning," she finally said, extending her hand for him to shake.

Finally, he thought, grasping her smaller fingers in his. A jolt of awareness ricocheted through him.

Her slight gasp told him she'd felt it too.

He raised a hand and brushed his thumb over her lower lip. Her eyes widened, and her mouth parted in surprise. Warm breath fluttered over his finger, and the sensation went straight to his groin.

He slid his hand over her cheek, cupping her jaw in his palm.

"You do things to me," he murmured, grazing her soft skin with his thumb.

She swallowed hard, her heavy-lidded gaze never leaving his. "You do the same to me."

Victory was sweet, but when he eased his mouth over hers, he remembered that she tasted even sweeter. He kissed one corner of her mouth then the other, enjoying the simple act of teasing her, her body's trembling reaction providing so much satisfaction.

He nipped her lower lip, and she curled her fingers tighter against his waist.

Her possessive grip only inflamed his desire. "I want you, Riley. I want to feel myself hard and hot inside you," he said, nipping her lower lip.

She moaned, swaying toward him. He caught her, wrapping an arm around her waist, turning the light kiss into a deeper one. Her tongue slid back and forth over his, her soft sighs rocking him to his core.

Somehow he maintained some sliver of rational thought, and with it came the knowledge that no matter how willing she seemed to be, any further and she'd convince herself to run. She'd withdraw before they tested just how good things between them could be.

So before he could act on impulse and take her against the wall, on her couch, or in her bed, he released her. Steadied her. Gave her a light kiss on the cheek, said good night, and walked out the door.

He'd convinced her to come to his turf. For now, that had to be enough.

FOUR

Riley drove to the stadium, her stomach churning in trepidation. Her nerves had already prevented her from eating breakfast, and it wasn't only the new job that had her feeling off-kilter. Neither was it the kiss she replayed over and over in her mind.

It was Ian, the man. He was so sure of himself and what he wanted. Such a dominant personality usually turned her off and would have, at the very least, had her resisting. And if he'd bulldozed his way into her life, she would have pushed back, but he somehow turned his insistence on getting his own way into a rational argument that had had her agreeing to the job before she'd even thought through her objections.

Then he'd turned what should have been a simple kiss into an all-out assault on her senses. He'd taken his time, teasing her, tasting her, arousing her, and bringing her to the brink of insanity with how much she'd wanted him inside her, hard and hot, just as he'd said. She shivered at the very thought.

She had no doubt in her mind that if he'd stripped off her clothes and taken her then and there, she would have gone along for the glorious ride. Her sex clenched with need, reminding her that instead of sleeping with her, he'd walked out, leaving her empty and aching. She squeezed her legs tighter, fighting against that rising need.

With a deep breath, she followed the directions to the stadium and pulled up to the guardhouse. She handed a uniformed man her license. He checked his list then printed and handed her a parking pass and directions before opening the gate with a welcoming smile. A few minutes later, she strode through the large parking lot, the May heat already coming up through the pavement.

By the time she reached the door, she was a sweaty mess, reminding her of the biggest drawback to living down south. She passed a bathroom and stopped into the ladies' room to pull herself together, blot her face and neck, and touch up her makeup. She assured herself the fact that she might see Ian had nothing to do with the extra prep.

A little while later, feeling better, she stepped out the door and ran directly into a hard body. She recognized the potent scent that lingered in her apartment and had kept her tossing and turning most of last night.

"Ian," she said, sounding too breathless for her liking.

He grasped her waist, steadying her. "You seem to be making this a habit," he said in an amused tone.

"Sorry." She bit down on her lip.

His heavy gaze followed her inadvertent reflex. "I'm not."

Neither was she, not that she'd be willing to admit it.

"I didn't know if I'd run into you or if I'd have to come seeking you out. Apparently luck is smiling on me this morning."

She smiled, relaxing. "Well, it's good to see a familiar face."

"Looking forward to your first day at work?"

"I'm nervous," she admitted.

He laughed. "Normal, but my sister's only an occasional slave driver. You'll be fine. Come. I'll show you where to find Olivia."

"Thank you. Better than me wandering around clueless."

He placed a hand on the small of her back as they walked down the hall. His touch radiated heat throughout her body, the neediness she'd fought to tamp down returning full force, as if her body recognized his, priming itself without her permission.

In the elevator, he stood across from her, watching her with pure lust in his smoky eyes. She attempted to distract herself by studying him here in his element. His dress shirt, a small navy check with white collar, and a complementing sky-colored tie brought out the blue in his eyes. The perfect cut of his suit accentuated his broad shoulders, making her wonder what his bare chest looked like, how much of a six pack he had, and whether he'd taste good when she ran her tongue down his chest, abdomen and lower, to the—

The elevator announced they'd reached their floor.

"After you," he said, gesturing for her to precede him with a gentlemanly wave and a knowing grin on his handsome face.

She stepped out onto the corporate level, certain the flush of arousal she'd experienced was obvious for all to see.

"Did you tell Alex about your new job opportunity?" he asked.

Oblivious to her thoughts, he led her down a long hall lined with oversized photographs of the team's best players decked out in full uniform.

"Not yet." She'd thought about it and decided to hold off. "I thought I'd wait until I had a specific position."

"You don't think he'll be upset you're working for the opposition, do you?"

"Don't you mean working for *you?*"

Ian shrugged. "That too."

All of the above had crossed her mind, had her wondering whether she shouldn't show up this morning as promised.

In the end, she'd been unable to resist the lure of opportunity any more than she'd been able to resist Ian so far. "Alex wants what's best for me. No matter what form that takes." But it didn't mean he'd be happy.

And if her best friend knew she'd kissed Ian again or that he clearly intended for them to end up in bed, their long-standing relationship would be in jeopardy. So she'd put off telling him. At least for now.

"We're here." Ian stopped at a closed wooden door with Olivia Dare's name on the brass plate beside it.

He knocked once and pushed open the door.

"Come on in," a female voice called.

"We already are," Ian said, his hand settling on Riley's lower back again as he escorted her into the room.

His touch was warm, hot, and felt too good. Because his sister was watching, she eased away from him.

"Olivia, this is Riley Taylor. I told you about her this morning."

The other woman rose from her desk. Tall like her brother and model thin, she was the opposite of Riley and her more petite body and full curves. If she hadn't come to peace with herself long ago, she'd be envious of Ian's sister.

"I'm so glad you're here," Olivia said, extending her hand, which Riley gratefully shook.

"I'm happy to be here myself."

"When Ian told me you'd be working here and I just needed to find the perfect fit, I was thrilled. Frankly, we need someone to jump between PR and Travel. Our travel secretary has the shingles, and he's out for who knows how long. An extra set of hands will be useful while booking for the season. Once things settle down, we can find a more permanent place for you. I hope that's okay?" Olivia asked, talking a mile a minute.

Pleased to be useful and not a burden imposed by Ian, she grinned. "I can handle anything you throw at me. I ran the distribution department at a sporting goods manufacturer. I'm used to glitches and problems and moving people and dates around."

"I knew you two would get along well," Ian said, sounding pleased. "I'll leave you to it." Ian started for the door then turned. "Olivia, do me a favor and invite Tyler, Scott, and Avery to my place on Sunday? Afternoon by the pool and dinner."

His sister nodded. "Sure thing."

"Add Sienna to the guest list."

Riley recognized Alex's sister's name and turned to stare. She knew how strained the relationship between Ian and the other side of the family was.

"Whoa. Did hell freeze over?" Olivia asked.

His mouth tightened. "No, I made a bargain with the devil." Ian's gaze slid from his sister's to Riley's, warming as their gazes made contact. "And it was worth it."

Riley shivered beneath his heated stare.

Olivia's eyes narrowed, catching Ian's not-subtle wink at Riley.

Just what kind of deal had he made and what did she have to do with it, Riley wondered.

"Why do I have the feeling the deal didn't include me doing your dirty work?" Olivia astutely asked.

Ian grinned, and Riley assumed he'd gotten his way with that smile many times in his life.

"I remember going to a certain party for you and Avery the other night, so…"

Olivia raised her hands in a gesture of defeat. "Fine. I'll invite them. Just add it to my to-do list," she said, grabbing a piece of paper and jotting something down.

"Add Alex and Jason too," Ian said, escaping out the door before Olivia could stop him.

"Argh! Brothers!" Olivia grumbled, lowering herself back into her seat. "They are such a pain in the ass."

Riley laughed. "I wouldn't know. Only child here."

"Well, my oldest brother is bossy, but maybe you know that already?"

"He's…persuasive," Riley said.

"And you're diplomatic. Anyway…" Olivia gestured to the chair across from her desk. "Have a seat. Relax. And we'll get you set up here."

A few hours later, Riley had been to HR, filled out paperwork, and found herself officially employed by the Miami Thunder organization. She was given a desk in a small side office, a computer and a password into the system, and her own instant message name within the company.

All the things a working girl could ask for. Best of all, she didn't feel like she was being given special treatment, which had worried her.

She was just about to sign out for the day when her message box blinked on her computer.

Ian: Hungry?

She laughed and typed back: Always

Ian: I'll come by and take you for dinner.

She wrinkled her nose at his bossiness.

Riley: That's not asking me if I want to go.

Ian: That's because I'm not asking. You're hungry, I'm hungry. We'll go get something together.

And there it was, the presumptuous side coming out. She swallowed hard, not liking the idea of being pushed.

Riley: It's been a long day. I planned to grab something at home.

Without warning, he stepped into her office. His shirt was unbuttoned, revealing an enticing expanse of tanned chest, his tie hanging loosely around his neck, and he'd slung his jacket over one arm, clearly finished for the day.

"Ready?" he said, looking more attractive than any man had a right to.

"I didn't say yes. I'm going home."

He frowned. "You have to eat, yes?"

"Well, yes, but—"

"Then let's go."

She meant to argue but somehow found herself being led to the parking lot, his possessive hand on her back. They stopped at the first spot, his name on the reserved sign. The lot had emptied out, and not many cars remained. A black Porsche waited for him there.

"Umm, my car is over there." She pointed in the direction of her vehicle.

He frowned, as if he hadn't thought of that. "Leave it here. We'll figure it out later."

"But—"

He hit his remote, the car beeped, and the doors unlocked. Before she could argue further, he nudged her toward the passenger side, and soon she was inside and buckled in. He was brilliant at getting his way, though she had to admit she hadn't fought all that hard. She wanted to be with him even if she didn't want him overriding her express wishes.

Enclosed in the small confines of the sports car, his cologne permeated every one of her senses. He took her to one of his favorite restaurants, an Italian place where the owner knew him by name and hovered to make sure he was satisfied with the meal and the service. To her surprise, time passed quickly with interesting chitchat and fun banter. Ian was good company, interested in everything she had to say. He asked a lot of questions about her life. Simple questions. He didn't dig deep, but she suspected he was merely biding his time. She was doing the same, satisfied to learn about him in small increments.

The pattern continued throughout the week. He'd show up to take her to dinner, not take no for an answer, and she'd invariably stopped arguing. His persistence endeared him to her even more. He didn't hide his interest, and she couldn't help but respond. Although he took their get-to-know-you dance slowly, he didn't mask his ultimate intent to wine, dine, and seduce her.

He was a tactile man, something she wasn't used to but quickly grew accustomed to and even desired. He always reserved them a booth and sat close by her side, his arm stretched behind her head, his big hand tangling in her curls. She felt the pull from her scalp to between her thighs, and it was all she could do not to attack him at the table. Especially when every single night he kissed her long, hot, and deep but ultimately sent her home, leaving her aroused and aching for so much more. She supposed that was his plan, and he was accomplishing it spectacularly.

How could she not want to be with him?

Alex came to mind, as he did when she was alone and not overwhelmed and seduced by Ian. She wanted—needed—to talk to him and make him understand the job and the relationship or whatever she was having with his half brother wasn't a betrayal. She couldn't control her feelings for Ian nor did she want to. But Alex was in LA on a promotional trip, and this conversation couldn't happen over the phone. He'd be back on the red-eye Friday night, and she'd tell him on Saturday. As an excuse, it was a legitimate one, and though she didn't relish the conversation, a part of her was relieved to put it off.

By the time the weekend rolled around, she was ready for anything, almost wishing he'd take that next step. He pulled up to Prime 112 and left his Porsche with the valet.

The hostess greeted him with a warm smile. "Mr. Dare, it's wonderful to see you. Your usual table?"

He inclined his head. "Thank you, Maria."

He'd reserved a table with a view but one that still afforded them privacy. With no booths, he still didn't sit across from her. Instead, he held out her chair then sat beside her.

Prime 112 was one of the more exclusive steak restaurants in Miami and not somewhere she'd been to before. "You're a steak man?" she asked when they were settled.

"I come here for the burgers," he said without looking at the menu.

She opened a large leather binder and looked through the options, her mouth watering at the array of choices. "Thirty dollars for a burger?" she couldn't help but ask.

"Kobe beef. It's the best."

Oh, really? She folded her arms across her chest and nodded. "Then I'll have the same." If the man was that crazy, she figured why not join him.

He eyed her with an indulgent expression she wasn't sure she appreciated.

"Order what you like. You don't have to eat a burger because I am. Or because you think it's one of the inexpensive options."

She curled her fingers around the menu. "I like hamburger," she said, fighting off the blush caused by him having figured her out.

"Good. My siblings agreed to come over on Sunday for dinner, so I'll put those burgers on the menu."

"I'm sure they'll appreciate that."

"But will you?"

She glanced up at him. "I won't be there."

He reached out, and when he covered her hand with his, she was surprised visible sparks didn't fly from the heat his touch generated.

"Yes, you will."

She decided it was time to explain a few things to him. "Just because you got your way this whole week and we've had dinner together every night doesn't mean you can say jump and I'll ask how high." She met his stare, wanting to him to understand she was serious.

Ian heard the insistence in Riley's voice and knew immediately she wasn't kidding. In business or in his personal life, he wasn't used to not getting his way. His usual MO would be to steamroll over the opposition, but Riley wasn't his adversary. He wanted to know her inside and out.

She was different from the other women he knew. She was independent. She had spunk. All qualities he appreciated because few women argued with what *he* wanted. Only his sisters came to mind. Which meant he had to change tactics or she'd bolt. To his shock, he found himself doing a rewind.

"Let me start over. Will you come to dinner on Sunday?" He inched closer. "Please?" He stroked the top of her soft hand with his rougher fingers.

She swallowed hard, her delicate throat moving up and down as she reacted to him.

"Don't you think the first time you meet with your siblings you should all be alone?" she asked.

Ian groaned at her accurate assessment. "Yes, you're probably right. But that doesn't mean I can do it." He stopped short of saying he needed her, but she'd be an ideal buffer between them. "I'd appreciate it if you'd come," he said, managing to hang on to his dignity.

She bit the inside of her cheek, clearly still uncertain. "I think I'd only cause more problems between you and Alex. Not to mention between me and Alex. I still have to tell him about the job."

Ian grimaced. He didn't want Alex getting in the way of his affair with this woman but was forced to acknowledge his half brother had been in her life first. Which meant Ian was going to have to give when it came to the other man. Didn't mean he had to like it.

"Talk to Alex and get back to me," he said, giving her more leeway in her decision than he wanted to.

"I—"

"Can I take your drink order?" a waiter asked, interrupting as he stepped up to the table.

"We need some time," Ian snapped at the man, his gaze never leaving Riley's. If he broke eye contact, she'd withdraw and say no.

The waiter walked away.

She leaned closer, her sweet scent kicking his awareness of her into even higher gear. "I'll talk to Alex if you tell me one thing."

He raised an eyebrow, amused that she gave as good as he did. "What is it?"

"The other day, with your sister, when you were talking about inviting your siblings, you said something about making a deal with the devil. You looked at me and said it was worth it. What did you mean?"

She was also perceptive. "Alex wouldn't share your contact information with me. To get it, I had to ask my father. He had...conditions."

She tilted her head. "Go on."

"In exchange for your address and phone number, I agreed to reach out to my half siblings."

She blinked, her gaze softening. "You did that for me?"

"I wanted to apologize for not returning your call. I needed to know what Alex meant when he said it was too late for me to help you."

She exhaled slowly, pursing her lips together as she blew out a long stream of air.

He'd been deliberately slow and methodical with her, taking his time. But he wanted nothing more than to taste those lips and plumb the depths of her warm, wet mouth. Throughout the week, he'd been hard most of the time, thinking about her in the same building, dying for a taste. At home, alone, he'd taken himself in hand. If he wanted her in bed, he had to keep to the plan and stop pushing her around, but it wasn't easy. He was who he was, and there was only so much he could temper. From the sudden warmth in her expression, he'd begun making headway.

"Look, you obviously know things between Alex's side of the family and mine are strained. I hoped you'd come on Sunday to ease the tension. You're friends with Alex and now you're—" Tread lightly, he warned himself.

"I'm what?" she asked, a smile lifting her lips.

"You're involved with me." Blunt but not so aggressive she'd bolt. All in all, he figured he'd handled that well.

She laughed, the sound brightening his evening. "Is that what you think? A couple of dinners and we're involved?"

"By Sunday when they all show up, we will be."

*   *   *

After a week of him wining and dining her, keeping a respectful distance while luring her in with his domineering personality and erotic kisses, Riley decided Ian Dare was too much. He epitomized danger wrapped in a too-appealing package.

She eyed him in the quiet that fell during coffee, using the time to compare him to past relationships, none of which were all that recent. Nobody piqued her interest the way he had. Probably because Riley's usual taste in men ran to the predictable and safe. Being raised by a bully determined to have his own way with no regard to the emotional destruction left in his wake, Riley made no apologies for choosing carefully. She was immune to hardened, take-charge men.

So she ought to be immune to Ian and his charm.

She wasn't.

She did, however, wonder just how charismatic her father had been toward her stepmother before she married him and, too late, had seen his other side. Riley mentally pursued that possibility and immediately discounted the notion that Douglas Taylor had ever come close to Ian Dare in charm. Though her father had clearly known how to hide his darker self, never in his lifetime had he been endearing. Her stepmother, Melissa, admitted she'd been drawn to his neediness during his hospitalization, a weakness in herself she'd made certain she got over after the divorce. She might have been seduced by his good looks, but his charm? Not so much.

To even think about putting Ian and her father in the same category was insulting, and Ian didn't deserve it. But that didn't mean he was *safe*.

No matter how strong her heart beat when he was near, no matter how wet her panties when he turned his focus solely her way, no matter...*what*, she thought, desperately trying to remind herself why she needed to keep her distance. Alex had already pointed out Ian's penchant for jumping from woman to woman. Wasn't that warning enough for her to stay away? It should have been, but when it came to this man, she feared she was fighting a losing battle.

"What's going on in that active mind of yours?" Ian asked over dessert.

"I'm thinking about you," she admitted, deciding straight-forward was the way to go.

He raised a brow, obviously surprised at her honest admission.

"I was just thinking about how bossy you can be."

"Because I insisted you order the Fried Oreos with French vanilla ice cream instead of the warm chocolate chunk cookies?" he asked with an amused smile.

She couldn't help but grin. "You know what I mean."

"I'm not going to apologize for who I am." He lifted her hand and threaded her fingers through his larger ones. "For you, though, I'm willing to…temper those impulses."

Her heart skipped a beat.

"Certain times, certain places, however, I expect you to let go of your inhibitions and enjoy it." His tone deepened, leaving no doubt to his meaning.

Just to be sure though… "What sort of places?" she asked.

"I expect you to give yourself over to me completely in bed. To do as I say without hesitation or question." He raised her hand and pressed a hot, open-mouthed kiss to her palm. "I promise you won't be disappointed."

Her breath shot out in one long stream of air, and dizzi-ness assaulted her both at his words and the silken slide of his tongue against her skin. Good God, she wanted to experience Ian just like this, at his most dominant. The thought of submitting to him physically and giving him complete control over her pleasure caused a rush of heated anticipation to fire her blood and crash through every one of her defenses against him.

She swallowed hard. "I—"

"Yes?"

Those mesmerizing eyes bored deeply into hers, filled with the kind of erotic promise she'd only dreamed about. "I want...I mean I need..." She didn't know what she meant to say. Every available thought was now centered where a throbbing pulse beat between her thighs.

In an instant, he'd focused all her awareness on sleeping with him. On what it would feel like to have him sliding deep inside of her and coaxing multiple orgasms from her sex-deprived body.

God, the man was potent. And completely irresistible.

"What do you say? Come home with me," he said. Asked.

She wasn't sure which, nor did she really care.

FIVE

Trembling with desire, Riley barely remembered the car ride back to Ian's place. He pulled into the driveway of the Ritz Condominiums. It came as no surprise to her that he lived in a place that offered all hotel amenities while being privately owned. He came around to her side of the car and took her hand, pulling her from the passenger seat. He maneuvered her close to him as they walked into the lobby, held her beside him as they took the elevator to the top floor. She was enveloped in his heady, seductive scent. His body heat spiked her own temperature, the neediness pulsing through her core adding to the anticipation of what was to come.

The ding of the elevator's arrival on his floor startled her. They stepped directly into his apartment, and the door closed shut behind them. Before she could take in her surroundings, he spun her around until her back hit the wall, and his mouth came down hard on hers.

His lips were firm and demanding, taking what he wanted and making her need everything he had to give. She could only wrap her arms around his neck and go along for the ride. His mouth tackled her with expertise, his tongue gliding over her lips, sliding inside.

She parted willingly, taking him in, and the moment his tongue touched hers, he let out a shuddering groan that told her exactly what she did to him. The ability to have a maddening effect on this tightly controlled man excited her, but the minute she slid her fingers into his hair, he broke the kiss.

Startled, she blinked up at him, wondering if disappointment showed on her face.

His eyes dark and needy, he met her gaze. "I need to see you come apart for me."

She let out a relieved breath and somehow managed a brief nod, wanting the same thing. Did he think she'd argue?

He took one of her hands and placed her palm against the wall, then did the same with the other. "And I can't do that if you're touching me," he said on a low growl that had her stomach churning with excitement. "Don't move."

She swallowed hard, her hands pressed against the wall, her heart threatening to beat out of her chest.

His gaze never leaving hers, he undid her blouse, one button, then the next, and the next, his large, tanned hands an erotic picture against the soft silk of her blouse. He took his time undressing her, the slow anticipation causing her nipples to peak and harden.

"I can't wait to see you naked," he said in a deep voice, easing the silk off her shoulders.

Her shirt fell to the floor in a soft whoosh, leaving her in a lacy bra and her black pencil skirt. He stared at her then, his searing gaze taking in her full breasts, so much more than the handful she always imagined most men preferred.

Her sex clenched, moisture soaking her panties.

"So damned hot," he muttered, staring.

She felt awkward standing before him half dressed, her hands pressed against the wall, waiting for him to make the next move. The urge to touch him, to participate, to undress him and see his magnificent body was strong.

Just as she was about to move, his words from earlier came back to her. *I expect you to give yourself over to me completely in bed. To do as I say without hesitation or question.*

So as his eyes dilated with approval, she let him look his fill. And as he did, his erection grew larger, thicker. She did that to him, and the knowledge empowered her, allowing her to remain still and in place.

"I've dreamed about the way you might taste. Are you sweet, Riley?" he asked, his voice gruff and sexy.

Her lips parted, but no words came out. She didn't think he expected an answer, not that she could provide one.

He reached out, pushing the cup of her bra beneath her breast, and tweaked her nipple, beginning a steady massage of one breast that felt so good she arched, pushing herself into his hand.

His touch was molten, branding her, and when he twisted her nipple, her sex pulsed with need, and dampness soaked her even more. Her breath came in short pants, and she squirmed in place, trying to squeeze her legs together to alleviate the empty, aching neediness he effortlessly created.

"No," he said in a sharp tone that had her obeying while, the throbbing in her clit intensified. "I told you not to move, and when you come, you're going to know it's me who brought you there."

A moan escaped her lips, and she flushed in embarrassment.

"You're so fucking perfect," he said, his hands moving to her other breast, giving it the same diligent treatment, rolling her nipple between his thumb and forefinger, watching her face as her hips bucked forward.

"I think it's time I find out if you taste as good as I imagined." He leaned down and sucked one distended nipple into his mouth.

Stars exploded in front of her eyes, and the ragged sound that escaped from her throat surprised even her. "Ian, please," she begged, gripping his arm in her hand.

"Back in place," he snapped, and her hands immediately hit the wall once more.

She wanted to touch him, hoped he'd allow her later. For now? He'd barely played with her breasts, and already she knew she'd do anything he demanded if only he'd give her the orgasm she desperately needed.

"Good girl," he said, turning his attention to her next breast. "Is this what you need?" He bit gently on her nipple, and a full-body tremor shook her so hard she was surprised her knees didn't give way.

"Holy shit," she muttered, eliciting a dark laugh from him before he licked around the throbbing peak.

"I have a question," she managed to ask.

He stroked her cheek with one hand, his touch so gentle and caring he took her breath away. "Ask away."

"Do I?"

"Do you what?" Ian asked, surprised by the hesitancy in her tone.

She swallowed, the muscles in her neck moving up and down, making Ian want to growl and mark her there. Something about this woman called to his deepest protective instincts. For all her bravado and independence, there was an innocence inside her that provided a counterbalance to his more jaded personality. From the minute he'd mentioned her giving him control in bed, her blue eyes had dilated and darkened with a need that matched the desire pulsing inside his veins. He'd known she would be the perfect counterpoint to his subtle need for control.

Looking at her now, dark curls wild around her face and shoulders, lips damp from his kisses, eyes wide with wonder, instinct told him he was right.

"You can ask me anything," he assured her.

"Do I taste as good as you thought?"

That one question nearly brought him to his knees. He swept her into his arms and headed for the bedroom, depositing her squarely in the middle of his king-sized, four-poster bed.

He came down over her, his arms bracketing her surprised face, and pressed a hard, hot kiss over her lips. "You." He kissed her again, more thoroughly this time. "Taste." He delved deeper, sweeping his tongue throughout her luscious, hot mouth. "So fucking good."

She moaned and wrapped herself around his neck, holding him close. And though normally he'd push back and take charge, her arms around him felt too good to worry about maintaining control and distance. He kissed her back, all the while maneuvering his fingers beneath her skirt and panties, pushing the garments down her hips and thighs, until she edged away so she could get rid of the damned annoying barrier herself.

Then he was facing heaven. Her almost-bare pussy, damp with her arousal, beckoned. He leaned in closer, breathing in her heated, feminine scent.

His cock hardened, and desire raced through him. He'd never been so impacted by a woman before.

"I need—" He bit back whatever he'd been about to say, unwilling to lay his feelings out for anyone.

Her lips turned upward, her expression one of pure acceptance.

She arched her lower body, her meaning clear. "Then take."

She humbled him, and he allowed himself the luxury of stroking the delicate folds with his fingertips before lowering his head for his first taste. One long, leisurely lap of his tongue around her swollen flesh. And with one stroke, he couldn't stop himself from taking more. With deliberate precision, he licked and soothed her all over. From her bare outer lips to her inner ones coated with desire, he made it his mission to tease and arouse.

She moaned and shifted beneath him until he held her down with his hands and continued to take her higher. He thrust one finger into her wet sheath and curled it forward.

"Ian!" She groaned his name at the same time he pressed hard against just the right spot to send her into ecstasy.

Her body trembled, and he continued the assault, pressing his tongue down hard on her clit. She cried out, her orgasm sweeping through her. She arched into it, rolling her hips against his mouth as she came.

His cock throbbed against his suit, the constriction of his clothing driving him insane. Especially since she didn't hold back the sounds of her pleasure as he brought her over the edge—and kept her there as long as possible, continuing to lick and caress her as she settled back down.

He released his grip and raised his head. A look down told him his thumbs had left dark imprints on her pale thighs, and damned if a part of him didn't take pride in the knowledge that he'd marked her.

He rose and stood at the side of the bed, making quick work of his tie, tossing it onto the mattress along with a condom he took from the nightstand drawer. His jacket and shirt hit the floor next, followed by his pants and boxer briefs. He gripped his erection, pumping his cock, wondering how the hell he'd ever take her slowly. He breathed in slowly, controlling a need for this woman that ran so deep he feared it might never go away.

No way in hell could he let her know it though. He might want to slide into her, watch her eyes glaze over with desire, and make long, slow love to her while she screamed his name, her fingertips scratching his back, her arms holding him tight. But he wouldn't do it. Couldn't. Not when he knew the cost of that kind of trust.

He eyed the tie on the bed, knowing what he intended to do and determined that she'd enjoy every minute. And so would he.

* * *

From her position on the bed, Riley took in Ian's oh-so-fine masculine form and let out a breathy sigh, not caring if her approval went to his head. He'd just given her the best orgasm of her life and her first with a guy who took his time to make sure she got what *she* needed before worrying about himself. That alone would make him a keeper, at least in her eyes, but she knew better than to put any stock in those kinds of hopes and dreams.

Great sex with Ian? *That* she wanted more of.

He stood at the side of the bed watching, eyes dilated with need. *For her.* He gripped his solid erection and slid his hand up and down, pumping himself from base to head, as if getting ready.

She swallowed hard, suddenly nervous but determined to hold her own with this man. "Are you going to stand there or are you coming back to me?" she asked.

A sexy grin tipped his talented mouth. "Oh, I'm coming back to you all right." He pounced, his lean, hard body like a predator as he lay over her.

His chest hair brushed her sensitive nipples, his rock-hard abs pressed enticingly against her softer belly, and that massive erection teased her sex. A band of desire wound through her all over again despite having just come hard.

She knew better than to expect another orgasm and was beyond thrilled with the one she'd just had. Even so, at the idea of having him inside her, filling her, thrusting deep, she raised her hips in silent invitation.

He braced his hands on either side of her head and stared, a heated look in his gray eyes.

"You asked me if you tasted good, remember?" he said, breaking the sexually charged, silent spell that had woven between them.

She managed a nod.

"I want you to see for yourself."

Her eyes opened wide at the same time he kissed her, gliding his tongue into her mouth and twining with hers. He took his time, turning the kiss into a sensual experience, mimicking the thrust and retreat she was dying to experience with him thick and hard inside her body. He tasted like Ian, dark and delicious, with a hint of herself mixed in. It was the most erotic thing she'd ever experienced, and she tangled her tongue with his, inhaling the unique flavor.

Desire pulsed everywhere, and she wrapped her legs around his, needing to feel him. Suddenly he sat up, his groin flush with hers, and she moaned. He grasped one of her hands then the other. Before she knew what he planned, he'd shackled her wrists to the headboard with his tie.

"Ian?"

He stared down at her as if she were a meal he intended to devour.

She tugged but he'd managed to truss her up tightly. "Ian?" she asked again. Her voice quivered along with every nerve in her body.

Nobody had ever tied her up before. Nobody had suggested it.

"Relax." He spoke in an easy voice. "Give over," he said, reminding her of his earlier words.

She tried to swallow, but her mouth had grown dry. She ought to be afraid, but instead, the arousal she'd experienced when he'd instructed her to keep her hands flat against the wall returned full force. Dampness and a distinct pulsing began between her thighs.

She liked being bound? She wrinkled her nose, trying to understand her body's reaction.

"It's called submission," he said as if reading her mind. "You like being under my control."

"I do not."

His eyes narrowed. "Your body doesn't lie, sweetness." He slid his finger between moist folds, and her inner walls clenched, trying to capture his finger, bring him higher, harder, deeper.

He grinned.

She moaned at the emptiness she needed him to fill.

"Now that we understand each other…" He began to glide his body over hers, his thick length deliberately teasing her sensitive clit.

She shuddered and instinctively tried to reach out and hold him, to touch his massive shoulders and clutch at him while she rose to meet him. She hit immediate resistance, the knots he'd tied preventing her from moving, which, again, she found oddly arousing.

No, she thought, but bit back the words. He wanted this. She would try. Because she wanted to understand his need to control.

But she couldn't concentrate. Couldn't think about anything except the slick movement of his shaft against her clit, up and down, back and forth, harder and harder, until her hips began to rotate in time to the glide of his cock over her sex. His rhythm combined with the intense pressure, and a familiar need began to build deep inside.

She whimpered, needing more than the circular thrust of his hips and the hard press of his erection against her.

She needed him inside her now. "Ian, please." Her hips soared upward, but she was still empty.

"That's it, sweetness, give over," he said in a deep, compelling voice that oozed sex. "Feel my hard cock against your sweet pussy. Let yourself come for me."

The telltale tremors were just out of reach but so close, and she trembled, her pelvis thrusting upward, seeking relief. He rocked his hips against hers, once, twice, the movement utter perfection, and the crescendo hit, the tremors wracking her body. She screamed—the orgasm was just so intense and almost perfect but not quite, because he wasn't inside her. She needed him there—

Just like that, he was gone.

"No!" She squirmed helplessly on the bed, fighting the bindings, angry at him for playing with her, when she heard the crinkling of a wrapper and closed her eyes in blessed relief.

"Easy." He stroked her cheek, and she turned into his touch, needing relief in whatever form he offered it.

She forced her eyes open, and he loomed over her. "Good girl," he said, his gaze dark and approving. "Eyes on me. I want you to know who is giving you pleasure."

"I'm pretty sure I know," she assured him, barely recognizing her raspy voice.

He grinned and tweaked her nipple. She arched into him once more.

"Next time you come, you do it with me inside you," he told her, his gaze never leaving hers as he positioned himself at her entrance and thrust home.

He filled her completely, and flashes of light danced in front of her eyes followed by the prickle of unexpected tears. Sex had never undone her like this before, and it scared her. Her feelings scared her. He'd made her come so many times she'd lost the barriers and walls she normally kept in place. That and he was big, and it had been so long since she'd been with a man, the unexpected sting took her by surprise. And that was the only part of the story she planned to tell her-self—and him.

Ian caught the sheen in her eyes and stilled. "Shit."

He started to pull out, and she clamped her body around his.

"Don't," she said, her eyes wide.

"I hurt you." The last thing he'd wanted to do.

She shook her head. "It's been awhile. I just need to breathe. And adjust. You're big," she said, turning away.

Ridiculous pride washed through him at her admission. He touched her cheek, turning her head back to him. "You should have told me."

"Ruin the mood and send you running before we got to the good stuff?" she asked lightly.

"The other stuff wasn't good?" he asked, holding himself stiff, waiting and watching her intently.

She rolled her eyes and laughed, a novel experience. A woman laughing while he was hard and thick inside her. Him wanting to smile too.

"No, Ian, it wasn't good. It was spectacular," she said on a little moan accompanied by a twist of her pelvis that pulled him deeper.

Still hot and moist, she was beyond ready for him, and he relaxed his arms and lowered his head, wrapping his mouth around one of her luscious nipples and teasing her until she began to writhe and moan beneath him.

"Oh my God, I think I'm going to—" She cried out and rolled against him, her orgasm crashing over her from the suction of him suckling on her breast.

She was even more slippery now and completely ready, and he began a steady pumping of his hips, taking her hard and fast. She writhed against him, her climax seeming to never end, or maybe she'd just peaked again.

He only knew he'd never had this depth of want or need. He had to have her, take her, own all of her, and he did, with a hard thrust of his cock in her warm flesh, pushing deeper each time he pulled out then slid back inside.

"Ian!"

The sound of his name inflamed his desire.

Need, want, and something very much like emotion overloaded inside him. He took her with deliberate near-punishing thrusts that she accepted and matched by arching her hips in time to his. It didn't take long; he'd been close since watching her come so many times. His balls drew up tight, and the sudden explosion detonated inside him as he came harder than ever before. He continued to jerk against her until he had no energy left. No thoughts, nothing.

He collapsed on top of her, his body soaking in sweat, hers damp beneath him. Their ragged breathing was the only sound echoing in his ears when reality came back to him. He'd taken her like a man possessed, never stopping to ask if she was okay.

Cursing himself, he reached up and loosened the bindings, slowly lowering her arms and massaging her gently. "Okay?" he managed to ask.

"Mmm," was her only reply.

He made sure she could easily lower her arms and was comfortable before wrapping himself around her and cocooning her in warmth. Not something he usually did, but then again, his typical woman knew he wasn't spending the night in her apartment, and he'd never brought a woman here before.

Time passed, and she breathed easier in his embrace, where, he realized, he liked holding her. His heart beat harder inside his chest. It wasn't good for him to want so much from someone not in his immediate family. He knew this. The outside world tended to disappoint. Hell, his own blood had let him down.

But he couldn't help needing her beside him, at least for now, and that meant making sure that she didn't wake up, remember that he'd tied her up and taken her hard, and get angry and upset. Better to know how she was feeling about things now.

"Riley?"

"Tired," she murmured and snuggled closer, not farther away.

Her lush body pressed against him, making him hard all over again, so he counted down from one hundred, trying to sleep as she was obviously doing, breathing easily beside him.

Ian groaned, resigned to a long, sleepless night.

SIX

Sunlight woke Riley, the bright light on her face unusual when she normally pulled her shades shut before going to bed. She blinked, felt a hard body wrapped around her, realized she was nude, and last night came flooding back in stark, erotic detail. Her independent nature ought to be horrified at how Ian had dominated her, directed every movement up through when she could come, and yet the very thought had her sex pulsing with need.

Needing to see him, she rolled over and stared at his handsome face, so much more relaxed in sleep. She wondered what made him need to control every part of his life, including sex, as much as she wondered why she'd liked it so much. She wriggled backwards, and his hot, thick erection nudged her behind.

She held herself still and waited, but he didn't seem to wake up. She grinned and decided that while he slept, she could do a little dominating of her own.

He seemed to be a heavy sleeper, and she took advantage, slowly pulling the covers off and scooting lower. She cupped her hand around his already-hard erection, marveling in the smooth feel of his thick length, pulsing in her palm. Though she ought to keep an eye on his face to see if he woke, she couldn't tear her gaze from the sight of her small hand wrapped around him.

She slid her hand up to the head, down to the bottom, and up again, and was rewarded to see moisture seep from the top. She leaned down and licked him. His hips flexed, and she opened her mouth, enclosing him inside. She knew he was big from the soreness between her thighs this morning, and trying to take him completely was a challenge.

One she welcomed. She was nothing if not determined, and she moistened his length as best she could, licking him up and down then using her hand for better friction. She picked up a rhythm she liked, and apparently so did he because he let out a low, shuddering groan.

She peeked up at him without releasing him from her mouth. His head was propped on pillows, eyes dark and glittering as he watched her. She trembled at the sexy sight and bent back to her task, taking him as deeply as she could, twisting with her wrist, licking with her tongue, and deliberately teasing the round head.

He thrust upward, causing him to hit the back of her throat, and she gagged but managed to breathe through her nose and keep up with his sudden take-over. She shouldn't be surprised, she thought, as he began to pump into her mouth with a steady rhythm.

Deep, sexy sounds came from him and sent her body into a full state of arousal.

Unable to take it, she slid her free hand down to her clit and stroked her wet flesh, needing more pressure than she was able to give herself if she wanted to come. And she did, badly.

So did he, his thrusting getting harder and faster, and she wanted his release to happen in her mouth, to know she could cause this tightly controlled man to unravel. Her finger worked her clit harder.

Without warning, he reared up, grasped her beneath her arms and flipped her onto her back, looming over her. His hair was mussed, razor stubble added a rakish air to his face, and the effect was even more potent than when he came at her in businessman mode. And his damp, hot erection pulsed against her stomach.

"What are you doing?" he asked in a gruff voice.

"You don't know? And here I thought you had so much more experience than me," she said, feeling irreverent but also ready.

His eyes darkened. "Funny."

"Let me finish."

"Not if you make yourself come. Your orgasms belong to me."

At his words, her nipples hardened, and moisture trickled between her thighs. She swallowed back a moan. "So what do you suggest?" she asked, unwilling to forgo her own pleasure just because he said so.

A grin passed his lips. Next thing she knew, he'd rolled her to her side while he flipped positions. He lay propped on one elbow, his face level with her needy sex while his erection protruded from his thighs, inches from her mouth.

"Oh God." This position was so...intimate.

Without giving her time to think, he leaned in and licked her clit. She shuddered and arched her lower body toward him. As if reading her mind, he grasped her waist and buried his face between her thighs. His breath was warm, his tongue wicked and so talented as he began to tease her, tempt her, and make her feel like she was losing her mind.

It would be so easy to shut her eyes and just take, but that wasn't what she wanted. She'd started this needing to dominate him in some way, and she intended to hang on to her sanity long enough to wrest some of his precious control away from him.

She held him, opened her mouth, and took his erection again, wrapping her lips tighter around him and pulling him deep, using as much suction as she could to work him into as much of a frenzy as he was doing to her.

He'd gone from lapping at her like she was the tastiest treat to teasing her clit, pressing hard, suckling the hard nub with tongue and teeth. She bucked against his mouth, and he clutched her hips in an almost brutal grip, holding her in place as his tongue slid inside her and mimicked actual sex.

He thrust his shaft into her mouth, over and over, and she moaned around his thickening erection. The sound had unintended results. He jerked, and he pumped himself into her willing mouth while she played him as best she could with her tongue and one free hand. He let out a long groan, and suddenly she understood just what she'd done to him, as she felt the vibrations straight through her core.

The tremors triggered her sudden release, and her entire body caught fire as she came, shaking and moaning around his thickening shaft, her release imminent. He nipped at her clit, and she shattered completely at the same moment he came in her mouth, hot spurts seeping down her throat as she struggled to swallow and keep up with him—and with herself.

*   *   *

Holy shit. Ian had just had his mind—and body—blown by a sexy woman who knew her own mind and refused to roll over and let him have his way. She demanded her due. And he'd loved it. Just as he'd loved sleeping with her in his arms and waking up with her lips wrapped around his cock. He was falling for her in a way he'd never let himself before, and it scared the living daylights out of him. He didn't like giving anyone power over him in any way. Most especially when it came to his emotions.

Do not overthink this, he warned himself. It was one night with a gorgeous woman.

He pulled himself up to the head of the bed and found her facedown sprawled across the bed. He brushed her hair from her face.

"I think I died and went to heaven," she muttered without opening her eyes.

He burst out laughing, enjoying her immensely. "Happy to have taken you there."

He took her in, gorgeous curls spilling over her back, her hips wide and generous, her ass perfectly round, and grinned at the sight.

"Come on, sweetness. Time to shower."

"Can't move."

He headed for his bathroom and pulled out two towels then turned on the shower so it would get hot before returning to the bed.

"Shower," he said, more forcefully this time.

When she didn't move, he debated only briefly then reached out and swatted her ass with his palm.

"Hey!" She raised her head and glared at him, but there wasn't anger in her blue eyes, only heat and sudden awareness and arousal.

He filed the knowledge away for another time.

"Come on." He scooped her into his arms and headed for the steam-filled bathroom.

Needless to say, the shower took longer than it would have if they'd just washed up and was one of the more memorable mornings he'd spent in a good, long while.

*   *   *

Riley normally avoided the *walk of shame*. It was easy when her boyfriends were few and far between, and one-night stands didn't happen in her life. Now she had to put on last night's clothes and ask Ian to take her to the stadium to get her car. All she wanted to do was escape the rest of the morning without undue embarrassment.

In the light of day, everything they'd done came back to her in vivid detail, and she didn't know how she'd face him. Where was the bravery she'd woken up with? Gone, now that his arms were no longer wrapped securely around her and she didn't know where they stood.

She stepped out of the bathroom to an empty bedroom. Ian had excused himself to take a business call, and apparently he still hadn't returned. She'd check her own cell, but she'd left it, along with her purse, in Ian's car.

Ignoring her rumbling stomach, she picked up her panties from the floor and turned them inside out, pulling them on. She folded her arms across her bare chest and groaned. Her shirt and bra were on the floor somewhere in the front hall, and no way would she parade through his big apartment naked. She'd have to find a dry towel to wrap around herself, she thought.

She glanced at the bed, surprised to find he'd left a folded tee-shirt for her to wear, and she gratefully pulled the over-sized garment on. It fell below her knees. She folded her skirt, tucking it beneath her arm.

She walked through the hallway, passing two closed doors, extra bedrooms, she assumed, and entered the main great-room area. She walked toward the sound of Ian's muffled voice and found him by the floor-to-ceiling windows overlooking the ocean.

He stood with one hand high on the window. Navy track pants rode low on his waist, and no shirt covered his incredible body, giving her a good look at his muscular back and arms.

She bit back a sigh at the sight.

Or maybe she didn't suppress it so well, because he turned around, and his steely gaze locked on hers. "Just take care of it," he bit out to whoever was on the other end and disconnected the call.

When he faced her, his expression softened. "Hungry?" he asked.

She swallowed hard. "You don't have to feed me. But I do need you to take me back to my car. It's at the stadium, remember?"

Ian remembered. He also recognized a retreat when he saw one. Normally that was his job. He didn't like that she was so eager to escape.

Not when reality would give her reasons soon enough. Before that happened, he needed to lure her back from wherever she'd gone to emotionally protect herself.

"That's not an answer," he said. "I asked if you were hungry."

Her stomach answered for her, and a rosy flush stained her cheeks.

He laughed. "I thought so."

He wrapped an arm around her waist and led her to the kitchen, all the while, aware of her curves beneath his shirt and the fact that she wasn't wearing a bra. He knew because he'd placed her clothes in a bag for her to take home later.

"Come. Breakfast is waiting."

She eyed him warily, as if she suddenly didn't know what to make of him.

He felt the same way. Most women he slept with clung to him, hoping he'd find something about them that would make him interested longer. He often suspected it was his money that had them so enthralled, because he certainly didn't treat them to his charming personality the morning after, or feed them breakfast.

With subtle pressure on her back, he led her to the kitchen, where breakfast had been delivered while she finished in the bathroom. "Sit."

She chose a chair and settled into a seat, studying the spread of food laid out before them.

"I wasn't sure what you liked," he said. "I figured since one of the benefits of living here involves full room service, you might as well take your pick."

"Thank you." She picked up a bagel and spread cream cheese over it, ignoring the fruit.

He grinned. "A carb girl."

"I worked up an appetite." The blush returned. "I can eat it on the way to the stadium if you have things to do."

He slid his chair closer to her, gratified when her color heightened even more and her breath caught in her throat. He didn't want to be alone in feeling like he couldn't get enough of her.

Still, she was suddenly skittish, and he wanted to know why. "In a rush to get away?" he asked her.

"No, it's just...I don't know...I don't do this." She glanced away and took a large bite of her bagel.

"Define *this*."

She chewed and swallowed. "I don't usually have sex with a guy outside of a relationship."

Now they were getting somewhere. "And?" He needed her to continue with no suggestions from him. He wanted her unvarnished take on what this thing between them was. Because he was still working it out himself.

Without meeting his gaze, she took another bagel bite, chewed, swallowed, and followed it with a long sip of orange juice.

He waited.

"Alex said you go from woman to woman," she finally admitted.

He clenched his jaw, wanting to kill his half brother for offering any kind of take on his life. The other man didn't know him. At all.

"That's been my MO," he admitted to her.

She placed her unfinished bagel on the plate. "Well, I appreciate your honesty. Can we go now?"

He shook his head and couldn't stop the grin from spreading across his face. "Riley, Riley, Riley. I said that's *been* my MO. Has there been anything about my behavior, from last night to this morning, that led you to believe I'm finished with you?"

To punctuate his point, he swiped his finger over the corner of her lip, where a drop of cream cheese remained, and licked it off his finger while she watched. Her eyes dilated with undisguised need, and his cock grew harder in his sweats.

"So we're not finished?" She gripped her napkin in her lap, twisting it unmercifully.

"Not by a long shot."

She finally met his gaze. Big blue eyes stared at him through thick lashes, as she clearly worked out what she wanted to say next.

"I have some rules."

He raised an eyebrow, not wanting to be amused, yet he was, despite himself. "Go on."

She drew a deep breath and straightened her shoulders. "If you don't want to call this a relationship, that's fine, but if you're seeing me, you aren't seeing other women at the same time."

He hadn't said he didn't consider them in a relationship. Hell, Ian wouldn't know what a relationship entailed, but he had a feeling that admission wouldn't win him any points.

He rested his hand on her thigh where his shirt had inched up, revealing bare skin. "We both know that since we started going out together, I haven't had time for anyone else. But you'll be happy to know I haven't wanted anyone either. So no other women." He stroked her soft flesh, inching higher with a broad sweep of his thumb.

"Good." Her voice came out on a husky rasp.

"Now for a condition of my own." He lifted her chin with his hand. "No other men for you."

"Done." A cheeky grin lifted her lips, and he knew he had her back.

No more distance.

He leaned in and brushed his lips over hers, tasting a mix of Riley and citrus from her juice.

She moaned and kissed him briefly before pulling away. "One more thing."

"What would that be?" he asked, enjoying her way too much.

"I have to tell Alex, and I have to do it my way. He won't be happy, and I need him to understand. I need him in my corner. That's nonnegotiable."

Ian closed his eyes and groaned, not because he objected to how she handled his half brother and her friend, but for far more serious reasons. "I think that may be a problem," he told her.

She stiffened and pulled back. "Ian, I said nonnegotiable, and I meant it. Alex isn't just my friend, he's my *family*." Her entire body trembled. "For a long time, he was the only person I had in my life who protected me." She flinched at her own words. Obviously she hadn't meant to reveal that much.

But she'd said it, and now he wondered. Protected her? From whom? There was a story there, Ian knew, and if they had time, he'd ask her about it.

"The point is, if you can't give me that then—"

"I'd give you time to talk to him if I could, but it's too late. That call I got this morning? It was about this."

He grabbed his iPhone from the counter, opened the email that had come in earlier, a link to a well-known sports blog that had posted a photo of the two of them taken last night as they exited the restaurant.

Her cheeks were flushed. Her hand in his. There was no doubt they were together. Or intended to be.

She took the phone and stared at the photo filling the screen. "Oh God." She jumped up from her seat.

"My phone. I need my phone from your car." She started for the door then turned back to him. "Why didn't you tell me about the picture before?"

"It's only been ten minutes since I found out. I was trying to find out how far it spread."

"And?" she asked.

"It's gone viral, in the Miami sports blogs anyway."

She winced. "What are they saying? What's the caption?"

"Is it important?" he asked, not wanting to get into *that*.

She eyed him warily. "The fact that you asked that tells me it is," she said in a cool voice.

He met her gaze. "Miami Thunder President, Ian Dare, and his latest fling. What are the odds this one makes it beyond the weekend?"

"Wonderful," she muttered.

He refused to lose her over something he couldn't control. "It only matters what goes on between us, and we've already had this conversation. You don't need to worry."

"It's not me I'm worried about," she said, her expression panic-stricken. "I need to call Alex."

Of course she did. Somehow he managed to stop the words from coming out of his mouth. "Use my phone," he said.

When she hesitated, he said, "It's faster than waiting for my car to be brought around."

She swallowed hard. "Thanks." She dialed and waited for the other man to answer.

Ian knew he ought to give her privacy, but he couldn't bring himself to walk out. He didn't like being in the dark, and when it came to Riley and Alex, he wasn't just the one being blacked out, he was entirely on the outside looking in. The thought turned his stomach.

"Hi, it's me," she said.

"Dammit, Riley—I've been calling you all night. Then I wake up this morning to that photo of you and Ian?"

Ian stood close enough to Riley that Alex's voice carried from the other end, and he clenched his hands at his sides.

"I was waiting until you came home from your trip to tell you in person." She glanced at Ian and turned away. "He offered me a job with the Thunder."

"And he's fucking you at the same time?" Alex yelled.

"It's not like that!" she shot right back.

Except it was exactly like that, Ian thought, and they both knew it.

"You're home from LA, right?" she asked.

Whatever his answer, he'd lowered his voice, and Ian could no longer hear.

"Okay then. I'll see you this afternoon. In the meantime, calm down." Silence followed, then, "Love you too. Bye."

Resisting the urge to punch something, Ian waited for her to turn back toward him. When she did, she appeared much more subdued than he'd have liked.

"He hates me that much?" Ian asked her.

She shook her head. "No matter what he said, it's not all about you. It's about me and Alex. And me keeping this from him for the last week."

"You said he's your family."

She looked up at him, eyes wide and glassy. "He is. Alex and my stepmom. They're all I have."

Ian wanted to be included in that short list. It didn't matter how little he really knew her, what he did know had only convinced him she was special. The right person for him in an otherwise empty personal life. Other than family, who he'd do anything for, he hadn't had anyone he'd felt so strongly for—ever. Losing her before they ever got started wasn't an option.

"What about your parents?"

She swallowed hard. "My mom died when I was sixteen. And my father...I don't have a relationship with him, and I don't discuss him. Ever."

Ian accepted that declaration. For now.

"Can you take me to get my car?" she asked.

"Sure." The morning had imploded in a way he'd never expected, and he saw no way of salvaging things.

Until she made her peace with Alex, no amount of coaxing by Ian would make things better. Which made Ian's overture to his half siblings tomorrow night that much more important.

SEVEN

Riley stripped out of her clothes and stepped into the shower, eager to wash away the stress of the day. But all the hot water in the world couldn't erase the knowledge that Alex wasn't pleased about her relationship with Ian. To say he hated it would be an understatement. He wouldn't stand in her way, but he couldn't say he was happy. He didn't trust his half brother, and she understood why.

From the time they were kids and Alex had found out he had an older brother, he'd been eager to get to know him. Someone to have his back, instead of him having to have theirs, as he did with his siblings. Ian had played football in high school, like Alex. Ian had gotten a scholarship to the University of Florida, like Alex. But no matter how many similarities the teenagers and then the men shared, Ian froze Alex and his family out.

It made sense, of course. Alex's sister Sienna and her childhood leukemia had exposed their father's affair with Alex's mother. Sienna had needed a bone marrow donor, and Robert Dare had revealed the truth in the hopes one of his other children would be a match. Avery had been, which had led to Avery, Olivia, and Sienna bonding during hospital time.

The sad thing was, Savannah had always known about Robert Dare's wife and kids. She'd accepted it because his marriage to Emma St. Claire had been one of convenience, while he'd loved Savannah. And though Alex had been an *oops* baby, their relationship had taken hold, and he'd built a family with them. Spent time with them. More time than he had with his real family.

So Sienna's illness had been the catalyst for destroying Ian's family. Of course he wanted nothing to do with the kids his father had with another woman. Even Alex rationally understood that, but as they grew to be adults, instead of getting beyond their father's mistakes, their competition only grew, with Alex being drafted by the Tampa Breakers, while Ian had already begun his climb within the Thunder organization. Just another rivalry to separate the men.

And now, just when Ian had reached out, Riley stood between the two men. Which meant she had to do whatever she could to make it possible for Alex to accept Ian's overture.

To start with, she wouldn't go to the Sunday dinner, giving them time together alone. And she would keep her distance from Ian until the two men got used to each other. Until then, she had no other choice but to pray they could learn to get along.

*   *   *

Although Riley had planned on eating at home on Sunday night, when her stepmother called and invited her for dinner, Riley had agreed to go. Anything to keep her mind off what was going on at Ian's between him and his half siblings. She worried the two men would come to blows as much as she worried they'd ignore each other and nothing would get worked out. Going out with Melissa meant she had something else to concentrate on.

Melissa chose Nobu, a sushi restaurant at the Shore Club on Collins Avenue. Riley dressed for the occasion, pulling on a white sundress with silver flat sandals and funky jewelry. Melissa picked her up and drove them to the restaurant.

The other woman had just returned from her honeymoon with her second husband, a neurosurgeon at University of Miami Medical Center. Her blonde hair was even lighter from the sun, her fair skin pink, her expression relaxed and happy. She looked younger than her years and always had.

They were escorted to their table in the center of a room with low lighting, surrounded by white curtains. Melissa ordered a glass of Chardonnay, Riley a club soda.

"So, how are you, *Mrs.* Masterson?" Riley asked, emphasizing the other woman's new title.

"Wonderful. I highly recommend it," Melissa said, beaming.

"What? The honeymoon or marrying a doctor?" Riley teased.

"Both." Melissa grinned. "And how are you?"

"I'm great." Riley forced a smile, not wanting to worry the other woman with her problems when she was so relaxed and happy.

Her stepmother pushed the menu aside without looking at it. "You never could lie to me, so don't start now. I can see the tightness in your expression. What's wrong?"

"I'd much rather hear about your cruise around the Greek islands than talk about myself."

Melissa narrowed her gaze. "That can wait. What happened?" Her stepmother pinned her with a determined gaze. "How about I start with the photograph that made the rounds on the Internet yesterday?" she asked when Riley remained silent.

"Since when do you read sports blogs?" she asked.

"I don't. David does," she said of her new husband. "So...is there something you want to tell me?"

Riley winced, but Melissa had always been the best of both a mother and close friend, so she decided to confide in her. "I slept with Alex's half brother, Ian."

"Complicated."

She nodded. "Alex has always been there for me. He's hurt I'm working for Ian's sports team, hurt I kept it from him and—"

"Jealous maybe?" Melissa asked.

The waiter stopped by to take their order.

"Whatever you want. You're the sushi expert."

Once the order was placed, Melissa pinned Riley with a look that told her she wouldn't be dropping their previous conversation.

"I don't think he's jealous. We're just friends. We never thought of each other that way."

Her stepmom propped her chin in her hand. "I don't know. He's been protective of you ever since—"

"Protective isn't the same as having those kind of feelings. He just doesn't want me to get hurt."

"Would Ian hurt you?" Melissa asked, getting to the crux of the matter.

Riley blew out a long breath. "I don't know. He's such a contradiction. One minute he's bossy and telling me we're going for dinner, I need to do things his way, and he infuriates me." She omitted the fact that his dominance extended to the bedroom.

"And the next minute?" Melissa perceptively asked.

"The next I'm feeling completely cared for and…secure." Riley looked away, unable to meet the other woman's gaze.

Melissa was the strongest woman Riley knew, her role model in all things. When Riley's father had bullied Melissa, she'd pushed back, and when he'd turned on Riley, she'd left him for good. It was Melissa who'd taught Riley to be her own person.

As opposed to Riley's mother, who had been a too-loving, too-caring, and too-sweet woman. Although she'd loved Riley unconditionally and Riley still missed her, she was grateful she'd had Melissa's example to follow. And she found it difficult to remember her mom because, with those memories, she was forced to recall the physical and emotional abuse her male chauvinist father had heaped on them both and the meek way her mother had accepted it, becoming more subservient as the years passed. She shuddered at the very thought.

"Riley, where did you disappear to?" Melissa placed her hand over Riley's.

She swallowed hard. "Somewhere we both promised never to go again."

Melissa's bright smile faded. "Honey, don't think about your dad. You can't change him, so there's no reason to put yourself back there."

Riley shook her head. "I'm not. Well, not that way. I was just thinking how lucky I was that Dad married you."

Melissa reached out and grabbed her hand. "You're the one good thing that came out of that period of my life. You're my daughter, Riley. There's nothing you can't discuss with me.

So what is it about Ian that scares you? Because I can tell something does, and it's not all about Alex."

Amazed at how well her stepmother read her, Riley laughed. "You're pretty perceptive."

Melissa shrugged. And waited.

"Ian's need for control scares me. I'm afraid I'm so taken with him that by the time I realize he's like my father, it will be too late. And yet I know that's so wrong. Ian would never—" Riley choked up and waved her hand, indicating she needed time.

She hated, hated that after all these years, the memories could still shake her to her core.

Melissa squeezed her hand tighter. "Your instinct is everything. Honey, I knew. Deep down, when I look back at the days before we got together, I knew. He never made me feel safe and secure. Those are powerful words. So trust your instincts."

Riley nodded. "But there's still Alex's feelings to deal with, and he has every right to resent Ian. Not to trust him. And I trust Alex's instincts too."

"He could be too emotionally invested to see his half brother for who he really is," Melissa said rationally. "He can't tell you who to date as a condition for loving you or being there for you. That's not fair either."

Riley blinked at that. "You always make sense."

"School of hard knocks, honey. But remember there's always light at the end of the proverbial tunnel. Life brought me David." And Melissa beamed at the mention of her new husband.

Happy to have the topic of Alex and Ian behind her, she changed the subject to the other woman's honeymoon. This time, Melissa was only too happy to comply, and over the rest of their delicious dinner, she regaled Riley with stories of the Greek Islands, giving her a much-needed distraction.

*   *   *

Ian's siblings arrived at his apartment earlier than the others were due to show up. He appreciated their support. Without discussing it, they all knew how difficult today would be. Robert Dare's eight children had never been alone together in one room.

Yes, the girls had all gotten close but not the guys. Ian figured they all harbored their own resentments, but they'd agreed to come today.

"Hey, good call on the burgers," Tyler said, walking into the kitchen. "These are my favorite." He eyed the Kobe beef burgers piled on a chafing dish, French fries in a second tray. He reached out one hand.

"Hey!" Olivia swatted Ty before he could lift one and snag it for himself. "Wait for the company to arrive," she said, sounding a lot like their mother.

"Spoilsport," Ty grumbled. "I'm going back to watch some baseball with Scott."

"Grab a beer," Ian called out as Ty left the room.

Olivia laughed. "Men and their stomachs. You're so easily led around."

"Meanwhile, Avery's in with them, and that's where the chips are," Ian said.

"She always could keep up with the boys."

"You're no slouch yourself," he reminded her.

She grinned. "I have to tell you, this is quite a spread you've got here."

"I'm just doing my best to be a decent host."

"Or trying to impress a certain woman?" Olivia glanced around and grabbed a burger for herself, taking a bite before Ian could stop her.

He rolled his eyes at her audacity, though he shouldn't be shocked. He also wasn't about to touch the comment about Riley.

He'd had her in his bed, he'd been inside her body, and he wanted to go there again. Hell yes, he wanted to impress her.

And to do that, he needed her here.

He glanced at his watch. Not only were his half siblings late, so was Riley. His stomach churned, and he didn't think it was hunger.

He joined his siblings in front of the television, but as the next half hour passed with no company and no phone call or explanation, anger burned in his gut.

He walked into the living room and looked over the city, seeing the view of Miami that usually brought him peace. Not today.

"Hey."

He turned to see Avery coming up beside him. "Hi," she said, pulling him in for a hug.

"Hi, yourself." He kissed her forehead.

"I'm sure they'll be here soon," she said.

She'd always been the most naïve of them all, and he loved her for her innate goodness.

"I don't know. Maybe they wanted to make a point, and they did. They want nothing to do with me." How better to be obvious than to stand him up in front of his siblings?

She shook her head. "It's not like Sienna to just not show."

"Did you talk to her?" he asked.

She shook her head. "I was so excited she'd said yes when Olivia invited her, I called to talk. But she didn't get back to me. Which isn't like her."

"Alex," he muttered.

"What about him?" Avery asked.

Ian let out a rough exhale, thinking about his half brother and his feelings about Ian being with Riley. "He's not too happy with me right now. I wouldn't be surprised if he were behind everyone's no-show."

"Give it time. Alex isn't a bad person, Ian. He just—"

"I don't want to hear it," he bit out, cutting her off. Whatever justification she was going to make for how Alex hadn't had it easy either, Ian didn't want to know.

Avery nodded, looking up at him with sad eyes.

"I don't mean to take it out on you," he said. "Go hang with everyone. I'll be in soon."

"Just remember, you always have us." She hugged him again.

Because she was the youngest, he often forgot to take her seriously enough, but she was his sweet sister, and she had a big heart.

"Thanks." He squeezed her hand, and as she headed back to the family room to join their sister and brothers, he turned to the windows once more.

As more time passed, it became clear they weren't coming. The more Ian thought about it, the more he was sure Alex was responsible for his half siblings' rejections. The son of a bitch was pissed about Ian's relationship with Riley, and he was making his feelings known in the most conspicuous way possible. Although what Alex had to resent Ian for was beyond him.

As clear as day, he remembered the days after he'd found out about his father's *other* family. Ian had taken a friend's car his father wouldn't recognize and driven the two hours out of his hometown, wanting to see for himself. And sure enough, there was the father who had no time for Ian and his siblings, playing football on the front lawn with his other son.

With the memory vivid in Ian's mind, embarrassment and frustration rose larger inside him. Embarrassment that he'd gone to such extremes, ordering in an expensive menu, and opening his home, as well as himself, to Sienna, Alex, and Jason, only to be humiliated in front of the people he loved the most.

And if it wasn't enough that they all weren't here, where the hell was Riley? He'd made it clear he wanted her here. Thank God he hadn't outright told her he needed her to hold his hand through this damned thing or he'd feel even worse.

Once again, when a choice had to be made, Ian had lost out to his half brother.

*   *   *

Once home from dinner, Riley couldn't stop wondering how things had gone with Ian and Alex. She decided to check in with her friend, hoping he'd give her good news about how he and his half brother had made inroads in their relationship.

She dialed his cell, and Alex answered on the first ring. "Hey, Ri!"

She heard his teammates in the background and frowned. "Where are you?"

"Had some of the guys over."

"After you came home from Ian's?" she asked.

He laughed hard. "Are you kidding? Why the hell would I go over there? He screwed you—literally."

She cringed. "You're wasted."

"You could be too if you'd come party with us," he said.

She closed her eyes and groaned. For a man who stepped up when she needed him, he could also be such an overgrown child. The result of his big contract and the fact that his parents hadn't been all that strict.

"You waited years for an opening with your half brother," she said, trying to reason with Alex. "Why wouldn't you meet him halfway?"

"Be right back!" he called out to his friends.

She assumed he was going somewhere quiet, because the noise level surrounding him died down.

"Because I don't trust his motives. I don't trust him with you. What if he's using you to piss me off?"

She winced at the implication behind his words. "Flattering. Very flattering."

"You know what I mean! He doesn't deserve you. And the fact is, I don't fucking trust him, period."

Riley glanced heavenward. "You can't begin to know whether you can trust him until you get to know him. If you won't do it for yourself, do it for me."

Heavy silence followed, which meant, at the very least, he was listening.

"Don't know if I can do it, Ri."

Pain twisted her heart.

Although she hadn't known Ian long, she wasn't finished getting to know him. She didn't want to be. But she didn't want to lose Alex either. She couldn't imagine her life without him in it.

"How did the night go for your sisters?" she asked, hoping that at least Ian had made progress with the females on Alex's side of the family.

His answer sounded muffled.

"Say that again?" she asked, hoping she'd misheard.

"They didn't go to Ian's either," Alex said, sounding more subdued than earlier. Maybe because he'd heard in her voice how much this subject meant to her.

Riley shook her head, her throat full. She couldn't bring herself to ask Alex if he'd told his sisters not to go to Ian's either. She didn't want to know, didn't need another reason to be disappointed in him.

"Call me in the morning when you're sober," she said, unable to stay on the phone any longer.

"Riley, come on. Don't put him between us."

She shook her head. "You're the one doing that. Not me. Night, Alex." She hung up, her emotions veering all over the map.

From anger and disappointment at her best friend, to genuine worry about how Ian had handled their rejection. She'd promised herself she'd keep her distance, but knowing he'd extended himself to his *other* family, in a sense for her, she had to see him. To know if he was okay.

*   *   *

Riley drove to Ian's and left her car with the valet then approached the man sitting behind the desk to give her name. She wished she could go right up without him announcing her beforehand, but if she wanted to see Ian, she had no choice but to let him call ahead and get his permission.

"Riley Taylor to see Ian Dare," she said to the older, uniformed man.

He typed in her name. "You're on his list, Ms. Taylor. Go right up."

She narrowed her gaze, taken off guard, until she realized Ian had probably added her because he'd invited her to his family gathering. And she hadn't shown up either. Of course she'd counted on Alex and his attitude to provide the explanation for her—never thinking he wouldn't come and get his sisters to go along with him.

When the elevator let her off inside Ian's apartment, he was waiting for her, arms folded across his chest.

"A little late for the party, aren't you?" he asked in a sarcastic voice.

"I can explain."

"Don't bother," he told her.

"Ian!" a horrified female yelled at him.

Olivia, Riley thought, recognizing the other woman's voice. She should have realized Ian wouldn't be alone.

Olivia strode into the room from the direction of the kitchen. "Hi, Riley," she said, subdued.

"Who's here?" another woman asked from the other room.

"Come here, Avery. I want to introduce you to someone. Drag Scott and Tyler with you," Olivia called back.

"This is a waste of time," Ian said. "Riley's not staying."

Olivia scowled at him.

"What's up?" A younger version of Olivia joined them, equally as attractive.

"Riley, this is our sister, Avery."

Riley smiled at the other woman.

"Nice to meet you!" she said in return.

"Av, I think it's time we all get going." Olivia gave both Riley and Ian a pointed stare.

"Do I look like I'm leaving?" a tall, gorgeous man with dark hair strode in, raising his burger in his hand. "I'm just getting started."

"Take it to go," Avery said, obviously having picked up on her sister's meaning.

Riley appreciated the girls' attempts to give her and Ian some privacy.

Ignoring his sisters' request to leave, the taller brother stepped closer to Riley.

"What's up?" another man asked. He carried a beer.

Avery and Olivia let out a joint sigh.

If Riley weren't so upset, she'd laugh at the dynamics between these siblings. She only wished she had a close family like this.

"These two Neanderthals are our brothers, Scott and Tyler," Olivia said.

Riley studied them. Although they resembled Ian, they each had more playful qualities that were evident immediately by the twinkle in their gazes and the warmth in their faces. Ian at his most relaxed always looked tightly wound. His siblings had dark hair, but their eyes were bluer, and each was drop-dead good-looking. Damn, their parents made gorgeous kids, she thought.

"Nice to meet you," Riley said to them.

"Sorry to say hi and run," Olivia said, nudging one of her brothers in the ribs.

"Hi, Riley. I'm Tyler," he said, ignoring his sister. "And it's always nice to meet one of my brother's—"

"Shut up, Ty," Ian warned in a tone that Riley had never heard from him before.

Scott grinned, unfazed by his brother's anger. "I told you he was serious about this one."

Riley's gaze shot to Ian, whose expression remained passive and expressionless, at odds with the strain in every word he spoke.

"I'm sorry, but all my brothers can be such asses," Avery said. "It's nice to meet you, Riley. I just wish it was under more fun circumstances."

"I feel the same way," Riley murmured, liking this sister as well.

Ty walked up to Riley with a swagger that reminded her more of Alex than Ian. "I wish I'd met you first," he said with a charming grin.

Ian's growl told Riley he didn't like the attention his brother paid her even if he was still upset with her.

"Even if we'd have met first, I still think Ian's more my type."

Tyler let out a loud laugh, as did Scott.

"I like her," Scott called over his shoulder to Ian.

Riley managed a smile despite Ian's continued glare.

"Come on, guys. I'll make you doggie bags," Avery said to her brothers.

Olivia chatted with Riley while Ian bored holes into her with his hurt gaze. Her stomach churned at the thought of being alone with him, but if nothing else, she wanted the chance to explain.

A few minutes later, the sisters shepherded the grumbling men, packed-up burgers with them, out of Ian's apartment.

Before getting into the elevator with her siblings, Olivia paused by Riley's side. "He's hurting," she said softly.

"I didn't know they wouldn't show up." Riley spoke equally quietly.

Olivia studied her face. "I want to believe you—because I think you're the only one who can get through to him."

"What do you mean? You're all so close."

The other woman frowned.

"If you're going, then go," Ian said before Olivia could reply.

Olivia leaned in closer. "If you hurt my brother, I'm going to have to fire you, and that means we'll lose a damned good assistant."

"Is that my new title?" Riley asked, joking out loud when, deep down, she appreciated the other woman's protective nature. In fact, it reminded her of how she and Alex took care of each other.

Olivia laughed. "Actually your new title might be Assistant Travel Secretary, but we'll talk on Monday. Good luck here," she said, sobering, before she turned and walked into the elevator.

Riley waited until the doors shut behind them before turning to face Ian.

Alone.

He didn't look at her, and his rejection stung.

"Why are you here?" he asked.

She swallowed hard. "To explain why I didn't come earlier. I knew if I were here, I would only be a point of contention between you and Alex, so I stayed home. I thought if you got a chance to know each other, it would be easier for us to be together."

"But it didn't happen, did it?" he asked bitterly.

She'd had it with his attitude. She strode over to him, getting into his personal space. "I didn't know Alex wouldn't show," she said, her voice rising with her frustration.

He gritted his teeth. "I all but begged you to come today."

"I told you I'd talk to Alex, and I did. He was upset and distrustful. I thought things would go more smoothly if I wasn't here."

"You thought wrong."

She reached out and placed her hand on his arm. Her palm burned on contact. She wanted to get through to him. She needed him to understand.

"Ian, please."

When he didn't crack, she glanced away, her gaze falling on the mirror on the nearby wall. She saw herself, hand on his arm, pleading with him to forgive her for something she hadn't done intentionally. Suddenly the sight transformed, replaced in her mind by her mother on her knees, begging her father to forgive her for some minor transgression that wasn't worth the anger or emotion invested.

It always ended the same way. He'd backhand her hard, sending her sprawling—into the wall, onto the floor.

Nausea and panic swamped Riley, and she ripped her hand away from his arm. "You know what? Screw you, Ian." She took another step back, tremors shaking her body. "You obviously don't want me here, and I sure as hell don't need to beg you for anything."

She beat a hasty retreat for the elevator, pressing on the button over and over, willing the car to come faster. "Come on, come on," she muttered, unwilling to look over her shoulder at the man behind her.

EIGHT

Riley's outburst popped the bubble of anger that had been surrounding Ian all day. She stood at the elevator, pounding at the button in a panic, and his anger, which should never have been directed at her, dissipated, replaced by concern.

"Riley."

She ignored him.

The elevator door opened, and Ian bolted forward, grabbing her around the waist and yanking her back before she could step inside.

"Put me down!" She struggled, but he waited until the elevator door slid shut to do as she asked.

She spun to face him, fury on her expressive face.

"What the hell was that all about?" he asked.

"You tell me! I came here to check on you, and you treated me like persona non grata in front of your family."

Yes, he had. He'd never been so angry or hurt, and it made no sense. Why the hell did he care if his half siblings showed up or not when he hadn't wanted to invite them in the first place? He'd only done it to get Riley's address and phone number, and when she'd bailed too, he'd taken it as her choosing Alex over him. Which clarified his blinding anger, to camouflage the hurt.

But none of that explained why she'd suddenly freaked—because that's what she'd done. Yeah, he'd been an ass, but not enough for her to react that way. He knew she wouldn't budge until he gave in first.

"I'm sorry," he said.

Her eyes opened wide.

He was just as shocked by the words that came out of his mouth. Words he never used, because in his experience, they made him weak. With this woman, it seemed there was nothing he wouldn't do or say.

Needing space, he stalked over to the wet bar in the living room and poured himself a drink. Pausing for a long sip as the liquor burned down his throat, he studied her, seeing her for the first time tonight.

She wore a white, strappy dress that clung to her generous curves, her curls falling over her shoulders and down her back. Now that he'd regained his sanity, he wanted nothing more than to grab hold of all that gorgeous hair, pull her hard against him, lose himself in her warm, wet body, and forget that he'd allowed his half brother to get to him. Make her forget that he'd treated her so badly, but that wouldn't solve anything between them.

They'd both overreacted. He understood his own reactions, at least when it came to her. He still didn't understand hers, and the mystery of Riley remained.

"Are you okay?" he asked from his place across the room.

Riley drew a deep breath and nodded, still attempting to calm down, to assure herself that what she'd seen in the mirror hadn't been reality. She'd sworn she'd never be *that* woman, the one who needed a man so desperately she'd accept anything and everything he dished out.

She replayed the events of the last few minutes in her mind. He'd been cold and unforgiving, but she was the one who'd flipped out. He'd grabbed her, yes, but the minute she'd told him to take his hands off her, he had.

And he'd apologized.

Two things she'd never seen her father do.

Rationally she knew that people could argue and get past it, and that's all they'd done. Had an argument.

She swallowed hard and slowly crossed the room to where Ian stood. "I don't understand everything that just happened between us," she said truthfully.

He met her gaze, equal confusion in the gray depths. "I'm not so sure I get all of it myself." He gestured to the sofa, and she joined him, settling in with just a few inches of space between them.

They sat in silence for long minutes until Ian finally spoke. "I've been telling myself for years I want nothing to do with them."

She knew he was referring to his father's other children, and she nodded, wanting him to continue without interruption.

His chiseled features were hard as he spoke. "When my father offered your address and phone number in exchange for me reaching out to my half siblings, I grabbed the opportunity. I let him bribe me, and the *why* has been eating at me ever since."

"Maybe you really wanted an excuse to get to know them?" she suggested, thinking that deep down, Alex and Ian wanted the same thing.

He exhaled a harsh breath. "Yeah. And that's what's been bothering me. I don't want to want anything from them," he said, running a hand through his short hair.

"Why do you hate them so much?" she asked hesitantly. "The resentment for your father I understand. But Alex and his siblings are as much victims of circumstance as you and your sisters were."

"Because he chose them." Each word came out sharp and punctuated with pain. "And before you say it, I'm fully aware these aren't the thoughts of a rational adult."

Unable not to respond, she inched closer, clasping his hand in hers. "No, but they are the feelings of a wounded child."

He frowned at that. "I was an adult when we found out about them."

"About eighteen, right?"

He nodded.

"If you ask me, eighteen is very much an in-between age. You were entitled to the resentment."

He looked away, and she sensed him sorting through his thoughts.

"Graduations, birthdays, a broken arm, a burst appendix. We didn't have a father for any of those events. We thought he was too busy working, and not that it made it okay to miss out on so much, but it made sense. And I looked up to him because he had this strong work ethic, so he could provide for his family. For us."

She saw the child he'd been, idolizing his father, and her heart softened even more.

"It turns out," he went on, "even if he'd been working, he was living with them while he did. Because he loved Savannah, while my mother was just the marriage his parents had forced on him to keep the business running." He leaned his head back against the sofa, his emotions running high.

She sighed, wishing there were words that would help, knowing there were none. She understood so much more about his side of things now.

"It makes sense you'd resent them. But it also makes sense that a part of you *wants* to be included in their family, especially since your sisters are close with Sienna."

He glanced at her, looking more the hurt young boy than the composed man she was used to seeing.

"Well, it doesn't matter, does it? Because Alex wants nothing to do with me."

"He'll come around." She hoped. Because the guilt was killing her.

But guilt and her best friend's disapproval didn't change her feelings for Ian, which were developing and growing stronger in a very short period of time. She was still shaken up by seeing shades of her parents in her interactions with Ian, but the facts weren't the same as her memories. And this revealing conversation showed her that even if she had flashbacks, she needed to remember to view Ian differently than she did her own father.

"And if he doesn't come around?" Ian asked, still on their conversation about Alex.

Riley knew what he was asking, and she didn't want to choose. She couldn't. "All I know is, right now, *I* want everything to do with you."

She rose and straddled him, her knees on either side of his waist, her sex directly over his now-thickening erection.

His hips surged upward, and he let out a low groan. "I know what you're doing."

"Really? Enlighten me."

He met her gaze, heat and desire simmering in the depths. "I spilled my guts, and now you're distracting me so you don't have to spill yours about what happened with you."

He was right, not that she'd admit it. "Today wasn't about me." And she wasn't in the mood to revisit her childhood out loud, when she'd just gotten him beyond his, at least for now.

"That's a non-answer." He braced his hands on her waist, seemingly more himself.

"I don't want to dig into my past right now. Okay?"

His gaze sharpened. "What happened earlier had to do with your past?"

She hadn't meant to reveal even that much. Seeking a distraction, she ground down on his hard length, moaning when the sensations rushed through her, delicious waves of yearning that precipitated the building of a fast orgasm.

His fingers pressed deeper into her flesh, and her flimsy, lace panties grew wetter. Heat spread from her core throughout every part of her being.

"I will get to know you," he said, his words a definite warning.

Maybe so, but not right now. She slid her body away from his so there was enough space to give her room to ease her hand into the elastic waist of his pants and brush the head of his cock.

His erection jerked against her hand.

"Commando?" she asked, the very thought sending heat spiraling through her.

He shrugged, as if his lack of underwear were an everyday occurrence. "I sleep nude, might as well make life as easy as possible."

"I can't say I mind." She eased her fingers deeper so she could wrap them around his velvety, thick penis.

His hips bucked, his gaze darkened, and his erection grew even more solid beneath the firm grip of her hand. Knowing she could wreak havoc with his control caused a rush of pleasure to storm her senses. Her breasts throbbed with the need to be touched, but this wasn't about her.

She wanted to take his mind off his family's rejection. Make him feel better. Just make him *feel*.

She pulled his shirt up and off then leaned forward, placing her hands on his chest. She breathed in his heady masculine scent, wet her lips, then licked one firm nipple. The salty taste inflamed her senses, and she wanted more.

He shuddered and groaned. Encouraged, she ran her tongue around and around the rigid peak, losing herself in everything that was Ian. His hair-roughened chest beneath her palm, his hot skin, and his incredible taste had her shifting her lower body, but there was no relief to be found. Only building desire.

Instinct had her wanting to bite, and she nipped him with her teeth.

"Holy shit."

His fingers bit into her waist, and the edge of pain heightened her desire. Tightening her grip, she pumped her hand up and down his shaft. His cock thrust upward, and pre-come moistened her palm. He groaned, and with her lips still against his chest, his big body trembled.

"You feel so good in my hand. So hot and thick. So ready to come."

"I'm not going to let you play much longer," he warned her.

"You will," she said, squeezing his cock in her hand. "Want to know why?" She looked into his handsome face.

"Why?" he asked, his expression a mix of pleasure and pain.

"Because I'm asking you nicely."

He slid his hand into her hair, another warning his willing lack of control was coming to an end.

"Please let me make you feel good." She peppered soft kisses over his delicious skin, moving lower until her mouth hit the top of his pants.

She slid to the floor. "Please," she asked again, hooking her hands into his waistband and urging him to help her tug his pants down and off.

He met her gaze, and the turmoil she saw almost had her giving in, but she wanted this. Wanted to see this big, strong man give over to her this one time.

"You have control issues." She pinned him with what she hoped was her most serious gaze.

"That goes without saying."

She nodded. "After what you told me today, I think I understand why. You had everything you believed in stripped away from you, and you had to take over as the head of your family. Control makes you feel like you won't be hurt again," she said.

He shuddered, her words clearly hitting a nerve. She remained on her knees, waiting.

"I won't hurt you," she said in a soft voice. "Just trust me."

With a low oath, he stood and let his sweats fall to the floor. Pleasure and relief suffused her as he tossed them away and lowered himself back to the couch.

She slid her fingers up his thigh, her hand looking small and delicate next to him. She crawled up between his legs and studied his hot, thick length, sure he'd grown even bigger in the last few minutes.

Undeterred, she licked his shaft, up then down, coating him with moisture before taking him in deep. He was so hot, so big, she hoped she could do this, and continued to envelop him.

"Oh, fuck, baby." His hand gripped her hair hard. "You feel so good."

Moisture trickled from her sex. Doing this for him was making her even needier. She tightened her mouth around his shaft and began to draw her lips up and down, creating an intense suctioning she both heard and felt. Her jaw stretched, her eyes watered. She added her hand, the moisture provided by her mouth making for slick ease of movement.

He tugged at her scalp, and she felt the harsh pull in her clit. God, she wished she could touch herself, make herself come. She moaned around him, sucking him as deep as she could, until he nudged the back of her throat. Needing air, she quickly released him and breathed in deep before she slid her lips around him once more.

With a groan, he cupped the back of her head, holding on to her as he jerked his hips, forcing his cock into her open, waiting mouth.

This time, she moaned at the sensual assault, which overwhelmed her as she accepted all of him, including his dominant need. He pumped into her again and again, as out of control as she suddenly felt.

She slid her hand up and down his shaft faster, twisting her wrist, and driving him harder.

"Baby, time to move," he gritted out, tugging harder on her hair, surprising her by giving her a choice.

She didn't want one and clamped her lips tighter until, with a harsh shout, he spilled himself inside her mouth, and she accepted all of it. All of *him* as he released not just his passion but, she hoped, also the pain and hurt that had been building inside him all day.

Although she hadn't found her own physical release, Riley collapsed to the floor, spent from the emotions she'd put into this one act.

She was surprised when Ian lifted her in his arms and carried her to the bedroom, laying her down on his bed.

"Breathe," he told her.

She forced deep gulps of air into her lungs until finally, her breathing slowed. She curled against him, wanting nothing more than his arms around her, which he did without her asking.

"That was awesome, baby."

She'd pleased him, and she let a smile curve her lips.

He brushed her hair from her face and stared into her eyes. "Someday you'll open up to me."

She hadn't expected him to forget her outburst, but she'd hoped he wouldn't bring it up again so soon. Not wanting to engage in conversation, she sighed and laid her head against his chest, closing her eyes. She was too tired to even think, and thankfully, he didn't force the issue.

*　　*　　*

Ian held Riley while she slept. His emotions had settled down, in complete thanks to Riley. That was the effect she had on him, and he wasn't just talking about the intense blow job she'd given him. And it had been incredible. The best he'd ever had—because she'd been emotionally invested in him.

Please let me make you feel good. Her words had shredded his emotions, stripping him bare. She'd gotten into his head in a way no woman ever had. Because she cared. Not because he was wealthy and could give her gifts in return, not because she desired something from him, but because she wanted just him.

When he'd instinctively grabbed her hair, her low, throaty moan had reverberated around his cock as she sucked him in completely. She *liked* the bite of pain, the direction he gave. But he had no illusions that he'd been in control. And in that second when he'd been about to come, every instinct inside him had screamed at him to toss her over the sofa and take her hard and fast. To be the one in charge.

He couldn't.

Didn't.

Because she'd needed to finish what she'd started, to give to him. And now here he was, with a woman in his bed, holding her, caressing her hair, and fucking thinking about his feelings.

Gentleness didn't come naturally to him, but for her, this felt right. She was changing him, seeping inside him and altering him in ways he didn't recognize. Ways that scared him to his very soul. Because life didn't come with guarantees, and nothing about Riley promised she'd remain his.

*   *   *

Riley woke up surrounded in heat, Ian's strong arms wrapped securely around her. A glance at the clock on the nightstand told her it was nearly eleven p.m. She inhaled and smelled his delicious masculine scent. She wished she could remain in the safe cocoon of his arms and leave her problems behind. A scary thought, as last night returned in vivid detail.

She'd given guys blow jobs before. It always seemed to be a tit for tat kind of thing with most men, but she'd never *wanted* to give one to a man so badly.

She'd needed to take Ian into her mouth, to taste him, to give him the badly needed release of his stress and pain. He'd needed to see that someone in his life cared enough about him to put his feelings first. She'd wanted to be the one to show him he mattered.

What she hadn't anticipated was her own reaction to his need to control. He'd gripped her hair. Her breasts had throbbed. He'd pulled harder. She'd moaned. He'd cupped her head in his big hand, and she'd nearly come from the feeling of being restrained. The other night, he'd tied her to the headboard, and she'd come apart, harder and faster than ever before.

Hadn't her father held her mother down and beat her? Hadn't he dragged her across the room by her hair? So what did it say about Riley that she liked being dominated in any way?

She exhaled hard, a low groan escaping from her throat.

"You're awake?" he asked in a deep voice.

"Mmm-hmm. Did you sleep too?"

"No."

She blinked into the darkness. "You just stayed with me?"

His arms tightened around her. "Yes."

She didn't know what to make of that.

The silence reverberated around them until she decided she'd overstayed her welcome. Both for her own peace of mind and probably his.

"I should go," she said, beginning her slide out of bed.

"Don't."

She stilled. Her heart beat a staccato rhythm, panic filling her at the dichotomy she'd discovered within herself.

"Stay," he said, an underlying tremor in that one word.

Her instinct to soothe him overrode her own sense of fear, and she rolled to her side, facing him. Her next words didn't come easily. "You have to realize that we couldn't be more different."

He narrowed his gaze. "We've had enough dinners together for you to know we have plenty in common," he said.

She couldn't help but grin at his attempt to deliberately misunderstand her point. "You know what I mean."

"I do." His body stiffened, but he continued. "Clearly we've both got issues. But you're talking about my sexual needs, and that's your fear talking. You liked everything we've done together."

She had. And that was the problem. She couldn't accept it.

His domineering ways went against everything she wanted for herself. It reminded her too much of the emotional upheaval and painful childhood she'd left behind.

He leaned over and pressed his lips to hers with such extreme gentleness, tears formed in the corner of her eyes.

Despite everything inside her warning her to keep her distance, she responded, tension leaving her as he slid his tongue over her lips. She did the same, their mouths gliding back and forth.

For a long while, they lay side by side, just kissing. She lost herself in the taste of him, in his ability to give back to her in this simple but oh-so-effective way.

Her sex pulsed, heavy with need, her breasts grew tight with the need to be touched, yet he did nothing but explore her mouth with long, leisurely strokes of his tongue.

Even when she expected him to push further, when she gave him every indication she wanted more, he settled for seductive strokes of his tongue over her lips.

And later, when she said she needed to go home, he respected her wishes and walked her to her car, leaving her beyond disappointed he hadn't pushed for her to stay.

NINE

Monday morning, Riley learned what crisis management meant at the Thunder front offices. Over the weekend, the travel secretary had informed Olivia that he'd be retiring and not returning to work when he recovered from his illness. Dylan Rhodes, who Riley had met last week, had been promoted to his position. He'd immediately begun making inquiries into new hotels, wanting to do things differently than his predecessor. As a result, Riley had been given a crash course in what it took for a hotel to become one the Thunder would be willing to stay in while on the road.

Under his direction, she'd looked into each hotel's ability to accommodate team meeting space, the ability for their kitchens to meet the dietary needs of the players, and their willingness to block out whole floors, knowing full well they could end up with vacancies due to winter storms and travel delays.

As the workday eased into early evening, Riley was exhausted yet exhilarated. She loved her new job and the challenges that came with it. She came back from a bathroom break to find out that Olivia had left a message on her desk to come see her immediately.

She headed to the other woman's office. As she approached, the sound of raised voices told her this might not be the best time to interrupt.

"This isn't the change I want you to make!"

Riley recognized Ian's sharp tone.

"Well, travel isn't your domain, it's mine, and I'm making it," Olivia shot back.

Riley raised her hand, debating on whether or not to knock.

"He's a womanizing ass," Ian said.

"No, he's just single, and you're jealous. This is ridiculous. Go back to your office and let me do my job," Olivia said.

Figuring it was as good a time as any and not wanting to hear any more about Ian's possible jealousy, Riley knocked.

"Come in!" Olivia called out.

Riley pushed open the door, and the other woman smiled. "Thank God it's you."

"I got your message." She looked from Olivia's relieved expression to Ian's furious one. "But I can come back if this is a bad time."

"No, your timing is perfect. First, thank you for jumping into the void and helping Dylan. He's been extremely pleased with your work."

"Thank you."

Olivia smiled.

Ian watched their exchange in silence.

"Dylan asked that you be made his assistant, and I agreed. You two would be a good fit."

Ian let out low growl that startled Riley, and she turned, meeting his gaze. "Problem?" she asked.

He opened his mouth, but Olivia beat him to speaking. "Before you accept this job, you should know it involves travel."

"Really?" Riley had never been anywhere in or out of the United States. Even college had been local.

"Yes. You'd accompany the team on road trips, and since Dylan wants to make changes to the hotels when we're on the road, you'll need to continue your research in person."

Riley's eyes opened wide. "I'd get to go to places like San Diego?" she asked, naming just one of the cities in which she'd spoken to hotel managers today.

"Yes. And you'd have to leave today for Phoenix. If that's an issue, I understand but—"

"No! It's not a problem," she said, doing her best to remain professional and not jump up and down with glee over the opportunity.

Olivia's amused grin told her the other woman had caught on. "So it appeals to you?" she asked, shooting Ian a look Riley couldn't quite interpret.

"Oh my goodness, yes!"

"Great. So go home and pack. A car will pick you up around nine. You'll take a late flight so you can get to work first thing in the morning."

"Thank you for the opportunity." Riley grinned, turned, and headed out the door.

*   *   *

Ian started after Riley, but his sister's voice stopped him. "Don't do it."

He turned.

"Don't stop her, and don't take away her excitement by telling her you don't want her to take the job."

Ian curled his hands into a fist. "I've seen Rhodes hit on you at every event we run."

Olivia dipped her head. "That's between me and Dylan. It doesn't make him a womanizing pig."

"I don't want her traveling alone with him."

"That's not your choice to make! Did you see her face?"

He had. She was fucking glowing. But he wanted to be the one to put that look on her face, not a job.

"She wants this job, Ian. If you want any kind of relationship with her, you have to give her the freedom to make her own choices."

He didn't know what exactly he wanted with Riley except that he couldn't let her go. But the more he felt himself falling for her, the more the fear gnawing at him grew. He didn't trust her to stay with him, and that was the crux of his problem. That's why he wanted to manipulate the parameters of her job and keep her in his orbit and his alone.

Olivia's hand on his arm surprised him. "You give Avery and me freedom."

"Not easily," he muttered.

"Okay, maybe you try to meddle in our lives, but we kick your ass when you do. I have a feeling Riley will stand up to you the same way." She paused. "But here's the thing. We have to love you and stick by you because you're our brother. She doesn't."

"No shit." Did his sister really think she was helping him?

"I meant, she doesn't have to stay with you unless she wants to, so don't give her a reason to run. All I'm saying is, think carefully before you go all caveman on her, okay?"

He raised his eyebrows, thinking that if his sister knew just how caveman he'd considered going, she wouldn't use the term so lightly. He already had to share her with his half brother, something that threatened the very foundation of whatever they were building.

In his mind, he'd had the company jet fueled and ready to go so he could beat her to Arizona and be there for every moment she'd otherwise have been alone with Dylan Rhodes.

"I have to go." He started for the door, finished discussing his personal life with Olivia.

"What are you going to do?" she asked.

"Nothing." Until he figured out his next move.

⁎ ⁎ ⁎

Riley wondered if she'd hear from Ian before she left for Phoenix. His mood in Olivia's office had been off, and she assumed it had something to do with whatever they'd been arguing about.

She pushed Ian to the back of her mind and focused on her upcoming trip. She packed a mix of professional business clothes along with some casual wear. Olivia hadn't said how long she'd be gone, so she improvised with mix-and-match clothing.

She called Alex and her stepmom and let them know she'd be out of town for a couple of days. Alex, she knew, had returned to his Tampa place for the week, and she figured they could use the break. She hoped, upon his return to Miami, they could pick up a more rational conversation about his relationship with Ian. And hers.

She'd already decided a complete break from Ian wasn't what she wanted, but maybe this short time-out would be healthy for her too. Her head and her heart were torn over the best thing to do when it came to getting further involved with him. Her emotions pulled her inexorably toward him, but she worried about the intensity between them and the way he so easily provoked memories she preferred to leave buried.

Yet she related to him on so many levels, from his painful childhood to the way he kept himself isolated from everyone except those he really trusted. If she needed a tie-breaker, however, her body was all in. Especially after the way he'd treated her the other night, so gentle and giving, so at odds with the man she knew him to be.

For the next few days, she wanted to focus solely on business and proving herself to Dylan. Putting Ian out of her mind, she headed downstairs to wait for the car service to take her to the airport. She met Dylan at the gate. He was a good-looking man, tall, dark, and handsome with a goatee, something she'd never thought she'd appreciate, but on him, it worked.

On the long flight, they alternated between companionable silence and talk, some business, some more personal. She appreciated his sense of humor as well as his dedication to the team. He asked about her relationship with Olivia, and she got the distinct sense he had more than a passing interest in her.

Riley turned on her cell phone as they exited the plane, and Dylan did the same. At the baggage carousel, they waited for their luggage and, like most passengers, studied their phones and missed messages. Riley texted Melissa, letting her know she'd landed. She did the same for Alex.

There was no message from Ian, and she told herself not to be disappointed. But she was.

They were greeted at the hotel by the night manager, who assured them the owner would be there to meet with them the next morning. He led them to separate suites on the same floor, and Riley said good night before letting herself into the room.

She stepped into a room filled with flowers. Bright, colorful bouquets of various blooms. She released the breath she hadn't been aware of holding, but clearly she had—ever since she'd run out of Olivia's office and hadn't heard from Ian at all.

She picked up the envelope on the table and read the small card enclosed. *MISS ME.*

"Oh, I will," she murmured.

Though it was earlier in Arizona, it was still too late to call. She didn't want to wake him. But a text for him to receive when he woke in the morning would be okay.

Will miss you, but thanks for the flowers, I'll think of you often.

Then she pulled out her toiletry bag and headed to the bathroom and washed up. She put away a few items she didn't want to wrinkle and climbed into bed, exhausted.

As she plugged her phone in to charge overnight, the beep of a text sounded.

That's the point. Sleep well, sweetness.

She let out a sigh that sounded too much like contentment for her liking and fell asleep thinking about Ian.

She met Dylan early the next morning at the breakfast restaurant in the hotel. "Good morning," she said.

"Not so sure," the other man said.

Riley narrowed her gaze. He wasn't the cheerful, upbeat man she'd flown here with. "Not a morning person?" she asked.

"That's not it."

"Then what's wrong?"

He studied her, as if unsure whether to speak.

She wondered what had happened overnight. "Whatever it is, just say it."

"I hired you for this position because you jumped right in with enthusiasm, and I thought you'd be an asset."

"And suddenly I'm not?" She stiffened at the implication that things had changed.

"Not if it means having the president of the organization breathing down my neck."

Oh, no. No, no, no. Riley curled her hands around the handle of her oversized bag. "What did he say?"

Dylan's gaze assessed her. "I didn't realize you two had a personal relationship."

Heat rose to her cheeks. "That has nothing to do with my job."

"You're right. It shouldn't. And there's no company policy against it either. But Ian called me this morning. He made it perfectly clear I'm to keep things strictly business between us. In fact, I believe his words were, 'hands off.'"

She clenched her jaw until she saw stars. "I'm going to kill him."

"I worked hard for the opportunity to step into this position, and I don't want it jeopardized because the boss's girlfriend is my assistant."

She fought back the tears that threatened. "I can assure you that Ian won't be an issue." If she had to break up with him to ensure her job had nothing to do with her personal life, she would.

In fact, right now, she had no intention of speaking to the controlling son of a bitch ever again.

Dylan studied her for a long moment. "I like how you think and what you bring to the table. I just don't want trouble."

"You won't have any."

He nodded, seemingly assured. He dropped the subject, and they ate breakfast prior to their first meeting with the hotel owner.

Riley didn't taste her food, but she knew she had a long day ahead of her, and she forced herself to eat.

When she received a text from Ian, she ignored it. Phone calls? She hit decline. She deleted messages without listening to them, her anger only growing as the day went on.

The next two days passed in a blur of tours, meetings, and eating at each restaurant in the large hotel. They checked out the conference rooms to make sure they could accommodate pre-game summits; they needed an even larger area for a makeshift chapel, because many of the players and their spouses liked to attend services. They sat down with floor plans, examined the layouts, the suites, the regular rooms, and by the time the trip was over, Riley's head spun with information.

Good thing she'd taken copious notes to compare to the previous five years' accommodations, since she hadn't been around to see them herself. Dylan seemed pleased and said they'd have a meeting with the rest of the team back in Miami before making a final decision.

Exhausted by the time the car service took her home, she wanted nothing more than to climb into bed and sleep. The time difference would be messing with her system, and Dylan told her not to come in tomorrow.

She was only too happy to oblige.

* * *

Ian showed up at his mother's house in Weston, which had also been his childhood home. Personally, he didn't know why she still lived here when she could afford to move wherever she wanted. Anywhere wouldn't have the memories this place did.

He parked in the circular drive and let himself into the house.

His mother greeted him in the hallway, her eyes sparkling with pleasure. Emma Dare, with her dark hair, not a strand of gray, looked younger than her fifty years, and she was as beautiful inside as out.

"Ian! I'm so glad you came by."

He hugged her and kissed her cheek. "It's been awhile, I know."

She waved away his concern. "Draft time. I remember how crazy your uncle used to get before, during, and after. No worries."

Before and after Robert Dare had abandoned his real family, his brother, Paul, had been a permanent fixture.

Ian grinned at the mention of his uncle. "Have you heard from him?"

His mother smiled. "He's on an African Safari with Lou. I don't think he'll be in touch for a while."

Ian chuckled.

His uncle and his long-time partner had waited until Ian was ready to take over the reins before Paul retired and they took off to travel the world. Being gay wasn't the reason he treated Ian and his siblings like his own children, but the fact that Lou didn't want babies was. Paul loved Lou, and he had his nieces and nephews to spoil when they'd been younger, so he never felt as if he'd missed out. Ian was happy his uncle was enjoying his life.

Grasping his hand, his mother led him into her state-of-the-art kitchen. Recently remodeled to indulge her love of all things culinary, his mother now gave cooking classes. It was her way of establishing her independence and having something for herself, and Ian admired her for it.

He settled onto a barstool while his mother poured iced tea for them both.

"So what brings you by?" she asked.

"Nothing in particular."

She placed his glass in front of him. "This is your mother you're talking to. You don't show up in the middle of the week for *no reason.*"

He stared at the multicolored granite counter, the wash of colors forming an indistinct blur. He hated it, preferring things in bold colors with stark contrast. Kind of like his life, with distinct rules, everything having its place. Knowing what to expect let him breathe easier. Which explained his need for control, in all things.

"So your sisters tell me you met someone special," she said softly.

Ian let out a laugh. "They have big mouths."

"They're girls! The first thing they each did Sunday night was call me," she said, laughing. "Olivia thinks it's a good thing there's someone who won't take your crap. Her words," his mother said, amusement in her voice that he didn't appreciate.

But he could never be angry with her. The little brats he called his sisters were another story.

"Who is she?" his mother asked.

"Her name is Riley Taylor." He went on to bring his mother up-to-date on how he'd met Riley and her entanglement with Alex.

"Well, that hits right where you hurt," she said bluntly, as only a mother could.

"Yeah." And he still didn't understand Alex and Riley's connection.

Yes, they'd grown up as neighbors, but Riley and Alex had an unbreakable bond. Maybe if Ian understood what lay behind it, it would be easier for him to accept.

"Yet she's worth dealing with them? I mean, you've avoided doing so for all these years." Her eyes lit with questions.

Ian nodded. If there was one person he could confide in, it was his mother. "Yes. She is. And right now she's ignoring my calls." And texts.

Emma laughed at his obvious distress.

"Umm... What did you do?"

He raised his eyebrows. Normally with that look, his employees would go running.

His mother merely laughed again.

"What makes you think I did something?" he asked.

She shrugged. "Oh, I don't know. Why would she suddenly ignore you unless you upset her?"

He rolled his shoulders, the tension there painful. "I sent flowers to her hotel room." And told her to miss him because he sure as fuck missed her.

"And?"

He didn't want to admit to the next part and let out a frustrated groan. "I might have called and warned her boss to keep his hands to himself on their business trip."

She'd left him a message while he was in a meeting telling him in no uncertain terms that she was pissed and he'd gone too far. And she wasn't answering his return calls.

"Ian Carlton Dare, how could you!" his mother asked, wagging her finger in his face as if he were a child.

"You should hear the things he's said to Olivia! I was just making sure he understood that Riley was mine."

She shook her head, her blue eyes dancing with undisguised laughter. "Oh my God. You are impossible. First, Olivia and Dylan have history, not that it's any of your business."

Ian nearly fell off his stool. "How the hell would I know that?"

"You wouldn't! Your sisters don't want you to know anything about their love lives because you scare men away."

He narrowed his gaze but didn't touch that remark, mostly because it was true.

"You can't go around staking your claim like some caveman!" His mother's shoulders shook from trying to suppress laughter.

"Now you sound like Olivia," he muttered.

"Because she's right. I'm sure your Riley would be flattered by your attention if you didn't insert yourself into her work and diminish her in the eyes of her boss!"

"I didn't—"

"You did." A few seconds of silence passed before his mother continued. "Ian, honey, you can't ensure the people you love won't leave you. You just have to learn to trust."

And wasn't that the crux of all his problems in life, Ian thought wryly.

"Thanks for talking, Mom."

"Honey, there's nothing I wouldn't do for you."

He rose and pulled her into a hug. The scent of her perfume brought him back to childhood, evoking warm, pleasant memories. "I hope you and Riley can fix things. I'd like to meet her one day." Her eyes opened wide. "Are you bringing her to the fundraiser Saturday evening?"

"We'll see." He had to get her to talk to him again first.

TEN

Riley's first day back at work, she was on edge and not only because she'd have to deal with Ian. When she'd played her answering machine at home, she'd had numerous heavy breathing messages. The caller didn't say anything, but there was no doubt the messages were deliberate, not mistaken calls and hang-ups. They'd continued after her return, waking her in the middle of the night and early in the morning. As she had an unlisted number, yeah, she was rattled, to say the least.

She passed Angie, Dylan's secretary, and smiled. "Morning."

"Good morning. Riley, wait. I have a message for you," she said.

Riley paused at the other woman's desk. "I thought my calls went directly to voice mail," she said.

"Not since your promotion. I'm now your official go-to person." She grinned and handed her a pink message slip.

"Cool."

"You're telling me! I'm fairly new, and Dylan's my first important boss. Now I have you both." The young woman smiled.

"Well, thanks. I'll try not to work you too hard," she said wryly.

Riley continued on to her office and settled in. She placed her Starbucks cup on the desk and glanced at the message.

You owe me. Dad.

Full-blown shivers took over. Riley hadn't heard from her father in so many years she'd almost convinced herself he no longer existed. Like a bad dream or memory that surfaced occasionally, she'd banished him to the dark corners of her mind as often as she could. Suddenly, the hang-ups at home made sense.

Her first instinct was to call Alex, but that would only cause an explosion that might not be warranted. She had to think rationally and decide how to handle the man. Not that she wanted to handle him at all. The very thought had her hands shaking uncontrollably.

As for Ian, he'd probably be furious if he knew her own parent was harassing her. He worked himself up enough when he thought about another man even looking at her the wrong way. She still hadn't told him about her childhood, the fact that her father had abused her mother, or that he'd ever touched her. She rationalized her silence easily. She hated the man and the memories, and given the fact that he hadn't been in her life for so many years, she'd had no reason to bring him up before. As for these phone calls, she assumed they were probably meant to scare her. A power play of some sort, nothing more.

But her hands still shook, and she hated herself for the weakness. "Breathe," she reminded herself, pulling air in, forcing air out.

She hadn't spoken to her father since the day she and Melissa had moved out. The day Alex had nearly choked him to death and threatened him within an inch of his life. He'd been petrified of Alex and his bulk, bulging muscles, and raging fury, and he'd taken Alex's threat to harm him if he came near Riley again very seriously.

So why was he surfacing now?

Her desk phone rang, and she jumped in her seat. "Oh my God." She had to calm down. "Hello? Riley Taylor, speaking."

"Riley, it's Jeannie from HR. I need you to come sign some forms and confirm a few things about your new position."

"Of course. I'll see you in a few minutes." She left the paper on her desk, face down, so she didn't have to look at the reminder and went on about her day.

A little while later, Riley had a raise she was assured was commensurate with her position, but she'd never made this much money in her life. And she couldn't help but wonder if Ian was pulling strings again. Another thing to add to their conversation about his meddling, controlling ways, because Riley refused to be under any man's thumb again, a thought that only served to remind her that Douglas Taylor had resurfaced.

Determined to keep her mind on work while she was here, she pushed her father to the back of her thoughts, and she dug in to the proposal the hotel owners had faxed over this morning, as promised. She met with Dylan, sharing lunch in the conference room as they went through the pros and cons of each hotel in preparation for his meeting with Ian, Olivia, and the general manager. He offered to let her sit in and learn from the exchange of ideas. Once again, Riley realized how much she loved this job and how fortunate she'd been when Ian had taken an interest and handed her the opportunity.

Ian.

As the day drew to a close, she finally let her mind drift to and stay on him. He'd kept his distance, not stopping in to say hello, not instant messaging her. Clearly he'd gotten the point that she was extremely upset with him.

She bit the inside of her cheek, not amused by the irony—she missed him pestering her throughout the day. At this point, she was more than ready to see him.

She approached his office. His secretary had left for the day, so she knocked.

"Come in."

She pushed the door open and stepped inside, her breath catching at the sight of him after what felt like so long. Shirt unbuttoned, his tan chest peeking through, sleeves rolled up, his muscular forearms all a treat to her deprived senses.

And she couldn't mistake the relief that flickered in his gaze when he realized she'd come.

"Hi," she said into the silence.

He rose from his chair. "I didn't expect to see you."

She swallowed hard. "Yeah, well, I was upset with you."

He strode over and pushed the door shut behind her, turning the lock. "Talk to me," he said.

"Okay. You can't go around dictating orders to my boss about me. He'll never see me as someone he can look up to and trust with his accounts if he's worried about losing his job if he so much as looks at me the wrong way. Or, heaven forbid, touches me!"

"Did he? Touch you?"

"Ian!"

He braced his hands on her forearms and looked into her eyes. "Honestly, I'm kidding. I was out of line making that phone call."

She blinked, taking in his serious expression in search of signs of dementia. "Say that again?"

"I was out of line. I shouldn't have called Rhodes."

"Oh. I…thank you. I didn't expect that to go so easily."

He grinned. "Sometimes, I can admit I was wrong."

"Okay, so while I'm on a roll, about the salary with my new position…"

"I have no idea what you're talking about. I don't know who gets paid what unless I've done the actual hiring."

She eyed him warily.

"Don't look at me like that. It's true. Is the salary not enough? Because I can talk to Olivia—"

"No! It's already a raise from the job I started one week ago. If anything, it's too much. I just wanted to make sure you weren't manipulating anything to my benefit."

An adorable grin lifted his lips. "Finally, you accuse me of something I didn't do wrong."

She laughed.

"Because God forbid I give you a raise."

She rolled her eyes. "I get the point. I do."

"The salary's that much more than you were earning?" He raised an eyebrow in curiosity.

She nodded.

"Enough for you to move out of your unsafe apartment building?"

"Ian—"

"Consider it a quid pro quo. I'm doing my best to back off and behave for you. You can move into a safe apartment for my peace of mind."

"And you don't consider this you manipulating me?"

"I consider this me doing my very best by you." He spread his hands in front of him, silently asking her to trust him.

"Fine. I'll consider it. After I do the math. I want to pay off some of my student loans, and with a salary increase, I can start to do that."

He opened his mouth then immediately snapped it shut.

Whatever he'd been about to say, he'd obviously thought better of it. Which meant he was thinking. About her wants, needs, and feelings.

She grinned.

Without warning, he grasped her around the waist, pulled her toward him, and kissed her. Considering he'd gone against type and given in to what she needed, she forgave him for messing up while she was in Phoenix.

She was happy to be back in his arms and had no problem showing him. She kissed him back, settling her lips against his warm mouth. He stroked with his tongue, and her stomach fluttered in anticipation. Her sex swelled, need building without any care to their location. The desire to connect with him was that strong.

He lifted her, and she hooked her legs behind his waist, holding on as he carried her to his desk, easing her down, disregarding the papers strewn beneath her.

He lifted his head. His heavy-lidded gaze met hers, those deep eyes taking her in.

"I missed you," she said, threading her fingers through his hair and attempting to pull him back for more deep, lingering kisses.

He didn't listen. Instead, he looked down, watching as he slid his hands along her bare thighs and up her skirt until his thumbs came into contact with her moist flesh.

She moaned at the intimate touch.

"So fucking sexy," he said, obviously referring to her barely there thong.

He pushed the skirt around her waist, easing the flimsy material aside and baring her to his hungry gaze. He immediately began to play with her, teasing her feminine folds.

In another lifetime, she'd be embarrassed that her skirt was hiked high, her private parts exposed, but she couldn't make herself care, not when he was so diligently trying to please her.

He circled her outer lips with his finger, spreading her moisture over her sex, arousing her but never quite reaching the tiny nub that would bring her the most pleasure.

"I need to come." She bucked against his hand, urging him to move his fingertip closer to her aching center.

He grinned. "You do?"

He slid one finger inside her, still ignoring her clit. But as he pumped in and out, adding a second finger, she felt every erotic stretch and glide. Her nerve endings tingled, her need grew, and she threw her head back, arching into his hand.

"Harder, faster...something!" She yanked at his hair, realizing she could give as good as he did when he drove her this close without offering completion.

He chuckled, his eyes darkening, as he pulled his finger out of her body. Gaze on hers, he licked her juices from his fingers.

She followed the movement, surprised and oddly aroused.

"You know why I call you sweetness, right?" he asked, as he unbuckled his pants.

Throat dry, she shook her head to answer.

"Because you taste so damned sweet," he said, dropping his slacks to the floor.

His thick erection strained against his stomach, and her sex pulsed with gnawing hunger at the sight.

He grabbed a condom from his desk drawer, jolting her from aroused fog to horrified awareness.

"What the hell?" Just how many women did he take in his office, she wondered, the notion turning her cold.

"I bought them after you took the job," he said, stroking her cheek with his thumb in a calming gesture that had her turning her face into his hand.

She exhaled a relieved breath.

"Better?" he asked her.

She managed a nod.

"Good. Because I haven't brought women to my home, and I definitely don't have them in my office. You seem to be the exception to every damned rule I have."

Her entire body went lax with the admission.

He stepped forward and slid his cock along her center. The delicious friction had her releasing a sigh of pleasure, and a full shudder wracked her body.

He stepped back, donned the condom, and returned to her, giving her no time to think before he was poised at her entrance and thrust deep.

"Oh God." She felt him everywhere, and her inner walls clenched tighter around him to keep him in place.

"Baby, you're so damned tight."

She moaned, and he slid out then back in, picking up a pace guaranteed to take her up and over quickly.

She leaned back on her arms and braced as he pumped into her, punctuating every thrust into her body with a hot grind of his hips that hit her clit in just the right place. The sensations built, white noise roared in her ears, and her body gripped his, trying to unsuccessfully to hold him in place as he took her soaring.

Without warning, he reached between them and pinched her clit between his fingers. "Come, Riley. Now."

Her body responded to his command. She screamed and blew apart, pulsating waves of light and sensation taking her over. Her orgasm swept through her, clearly triggering his.

"Oh yeah." His hips slammed into hers, once, twice, and on the third time, his loud shout echoed in her ears as he came.

Ian's brain buzzed, overloaded with sensation as awareness returned. Still buried deep inside Riley's warm body, her pussy clamping tightly around him, he was in heaven and would do anything to keep her in his life.

Especially since his possessive feelings only grew each time she welcomed him inside her slick body. "You okay, sweetness?" He lifted his head and brushed her damp hair off her face.

She forced her beautiful blue eyes open. "That was incredible."

He laughed. "I was right there with you." With regret, he eased out of her and went to his private bathroom, returning to see her smooth her skirt down over her sexy legs.

She looked up, a pink flush on her cheeks. "I can't believe we did it in your office."

A swell of stupid masculine pride filled him at the reminder. "You can damned well plan to do it here again," he informed her, in case she was thinking this was a one-shot deal.

"We'll see." She raised an eyebrow at his dominant tone then turned to grab her purse.

"Wise guy." He reached out and smacked her ass.

She spun toward him, lips parted in surprise. But her eyes also dilated, telling him all he needed to know.

"Come home with me tonight," he said, wanting more time. A quick fuck in his office wasn't enough. He wanted hours to talk to her, listen to what she had to say, and then devour every inch of her delicious body.

But she shook her head, dispelling his plans. "I don't want everyone to see us coming to the office together tomorrow and know I'm sleeping with you."

"I don't give a damn who knows about us." This was the first time he'd wanted a relationship, and she was shooting him down.

He was in over his head and wasn't afraid to admit it. Remembering she needed him to hear her and listen, he forced a mental step back. "Why are you so against us?"

She frowned at him. "It's not us I'm against, it's how it looks. I just started here. If I arrive with you in your Porsche tomorrow, everyone will think you gave me the job because we're having sex. Dylan already knows because you all but threatened him if he touched me."

He scowled at the mention of the other man's name, but he didn't miss the sharp edge of panic in Riley's voice and knew he had to back off.

He'd spent the last few days struggling with uncertainty, a feeling he wasn't familiar with. But until he'd known how badly he'd blown things with her, he'd been on edge. Seeing her in his office, having her come to him, he knew he was damned lucky to be getting another chance. He might not know what the hell he was doing when it came to relationships, but he knew he didn't want to lose her for good.

Listening to her cues seemed like the best place to start. "Okay, fine."

She met his gaze, a stunned expression on her face followed by an appreciative smile.

His heartbeat sped up at the sight.

"Want to get dinner?" she asked, giving an invitation he hadn't expected.

"Sounds like a plan. And since you're willing to be seen with me, how about coming to the Juvenile Diabetes Fundraiser with me on Saturday night?" Why not push when he had an opening? "The team donates to the cause, and my whole family attends."

She narrowed her gaze. "It means a formal dress and heels, doesn't it?" she asked on a groan.

He took that as a yes and grinned.

He knew damned well he'd been given a second chance and planned to make the most of it.

For him, this woman was the whole package. Intelligent, funny, and she warmed him in places that had long been cold.

Not to mention, she didn't take his crap, which he admired; his money didn't impress her, which told him if she was sticking around, there must be something more about him she liked.

A damned good thing, since he liked her too.

*   *   *

The last thing Riley expected was for Olivia to invite her to go shopping for a dress to wear on Saturday night. She suspected that Ian had put his sister up to it, but since Riley didn't have anything except the red dress she'd worn the night she'd met Ian, and Olivia promised she had a place that would alter dresses quickly, Riley readily agreed. She also needed the distraction from her father's message and the hang-ups that continued to haunt her at home.

They left work midday on Friday and headed to a boutique off Collins Avenue. Although Riley had window-shopped in the area once or twice, she couldn't afford to buy anything here, but before she could mention her concern, Olivia whipped out a black credit card.

"Gotta love when my brother's feeling generous," she said with a grin.

"That's great for you but—"

"You think he's doing this just for me?" Olivia paused in the middle of the sidewalk, causing people to stop short and swerve around them as they walked.

She raised her Chanel sunglasses and met Riley's gaze. "This is for you. I'm just getting a side benefit. And before you argue with me, we're here, so we're going through with it."

A warm, fuzzy feeling floated through her, but the objection came just as quickly. "I can't accept—"

"Yes, you can. You aren't denying me this. Come on." Olivia grabbed Riley's hand and pulled her out of the oppressive heat and into the cool, air-conditioned store.

Over the next hour, Riley said *I can't accept this* so many times it had become her mantra for the day, but Olivia assured her she had to or risk insulting Ian, who'd never gone out of his way for a woman who wasn't in his family before. Olivia insisted that Riley meant something to her brother, and Riley wanted to believe her.

So in the end, although the money was never far from her mind, Riley did as Olivia instructed—she let go and enjoyed. How could she not, when Olivia was fun and happy and her attitude was contagious?

By the time they finished for the day, Riley owned a dress so high-end she didn't recognize the name of the designer, shoes so expensive the bill could pay her rent for two months, and a Judith Lieber purse in the shape of peacock, glittering with brightly colored jewels.

Before they parted for the evening, Olivia informed her she'd be picking her up first thing in the morning for part two of their excursion.

"Part two?"

The other woman grinned, her eyes glittering with excitement. "It's a surprise," she insisted in that tone that told Riley no amount of prodding would get her to reveal what she planned.

After shopping, Riley arrived home, arms loaded with packages. Her dress would be delivered by four p.m. tomorrow. Her phone was ringing as she fumbled for her keys. She found them, unlocked her door, and ran inside, dropping the bags onto the couch.

She grabbed for the receiver. "Hello?" she asked, out of breath.

Click.

Whoever it was hung up on her. "Dammit!"

Her mouth ran dry. Before she could think about it, the phone rang again.

Riley answered it, yelling into the receiver. "I swear to God, if you don't stop calling me, I'll—"

"Riley? What's wrong?"

"Alex?" Relieved, she lowered herself next to her purchases.

"Yeah. Talk to me."

She sighed. "Nothing. I just came home from shopping, and the phone was ringing, my hands were full…everything's fine."

"That's why you were threatening me before you even knew who was on the other end of the line?"

She swallowed hard. "I heard from my father," she said, knowing better than to lie to him.

Alex swore loudly. "What did he say?"

"He left a message with my secretary when I was out of town. The note just said, 'you owe me.'" She repeated the words written on the pink paper.

"I'll kill him."

"It's not worth it. You were a kid last time you dealt with him. You have a career to worry about now. Just stay away from him. Promise me. I'm sure he's all talk," Riley said, praying she was right.

It didn't make any sense. He'd been out of her life for years. Why surface now?

"Not making any promises. I'm still in Tampa, but I'll be back tomorrow. I'll see what I can dig up on your old man. See what he's been up to."

"Thanks, Alex." She opted not to argue with him.

Still shaken up, she knew better than to call Ian. He'd know immediately that something was wrong, so instead, she texted him her thanks for the dress and the rest of her new things.

He wrote back immediately. *Seeing you in them will be thanks enough.*

She smiled and managed to go to bed happy, but her dreams kept her tossing and turning and on edge. Her childhood wasn't a happy one, and she couldn't think of one good reason for her father to surface, or what he could imagine she owed him.

ELEVEN

The next morning, no sooner had Olivia picked up Riley than she informed her they were spending the day being pampered. She should have said pampered, massaged and hot-stoned, plucked, waxed, blow-dried, and made-up. Her nails and toes were soaked and perfectly painted, a far more perfect job than she did herself. Olivia, it seemed, treated herself to this often. For Riley, it was a brand-new experience, and she surprised herself by enjoying every minute.

Before she knew it, she was dressed and ready and allowing Ian's driver to help her into the limousine. Ian waited in the back seat, looking extremely handsome in his black tuxedo. Clothes didn't make this man; he was too imposing not to be noticed, no matter what he wore. But with his hair perfectly styled, his silver-gray eyes focused on her, he was every inch the man she couldn't get out of her mind...or, she feared, her heart.

"You take my breath away," he said, his eyes darkening with his words.

Never before had she been the focus of such intense scrutiny.

"Thank you," she murmured. "You look pretty hot yourself."

"I'm not the one they won't be able to take their eyes off of."

She ducked her head and felt herself blush.

He lifted her chin with one hand. "I'll be the luckiest man there tonight. I want you to know that."

He trailed a finger down her neck and across her collarbone, his touch intimate and seductive. Her nipples beaded, and she trembled.

"I think that dress needs a little something more." With his free hand, he reached behind him and held out a long box.

"Ian, no." She'd already compromised her usual beliefs by letting him buy her this dress and the shoes, not to mention the complete spa day.

His eyes lost some of their earlier sparkle. "Let me give you this, please. It makes me happy. I want you to have something that...when you wear it, you think of me."

She swallowed hard. "I always think of you."

"Then let me in." He leaned in and pressed his lips against that sweet spot behind her ear, and she let out a soft moan. "Let me do things for you." He took her hand and placed it on the box. "Please."

She could see and feel how much this meant to him. It was a gift, and she'd hurt him if she didn't accept it. "Okay."

His expression transformed, his pleased smile making her happy she'd given in.

He snapped open the box, revealing a delicate, teardrop-shaped, diamond necklace set in white gold.

She sucked in a breath, overwhelmed by the piece. It wasn't ostentatious or over-the-top. It didn't make a statement or scream money, though she had no doubt the item had cost him a lot. Instead, it was simple, elegant, and every inch something she'd not only pick out herself but wear. And not just tonight at the fundraising gala, but every day.

He'd chosen the perfect gift, picked with her taste and feelings in mind.

"It's beautiful," she whispered.

"You'll wear it?" he asked.

The vulnerability in the question touched her. "I'd be honored." She lifted her hair away from her neck and turned.

He placed the necklace on and hooked it in place.

She swiveled back to face him.

He smoothed her hair over her shoulders, surrounding the delicate piece of jewelry. "It's perfect. Just like you."

She opened her mouth to argue. She wasn't perfect, and she had the past to prove it. Her father's reemergence had never been far from her mind, and she'd wanted to hide it from Ian for as long as possible. But he obviously cared about her, and he was showing her in so many ways, which meant it was time to trust him with her secrets.

"Ian, I need to talk to you."

"Later." He pressed his mouth to hers, gliding his tongue over her lips, encouraging her to open for him.

His masculine taste flooded her senses. Her eyelashes fluttered closed, and she parted her lips, taking him in. He devoured her, kissing her as if she were the only thing that mattered. He gripped the back of her neck with one hand while he swirled his tongue in her mouth, round and round, over and over.

She returned the kiss, the fervor behind it, and the need they both shared, until the car came to a halt and a knock sounded at the side window.

Ian groaned and pulled back, his hand never leaving her nape, his forehead touching hers. His breathing ragged, he dragged in gulps of air while she did the same.

She reached for her small purse and took out the tiny mirror she'd fit in, somehow managing to wipe away the lipstick smudges and reapply. Her lips still looked puffy, her mouth well kissed, but there was nothing she could do about that.

She eyed Ian, dabbing at her lipstick marks on his lips and face until she'd cleaned him up too.

"We'll pick this up where we left off," he said, the promise in his voice as seductive as his kisses.

"I'll hold you to that." She managed a grin, ignoring the pulsing in her body and the niggling guilt that she was holding back about her father.

Why that had suddenly begun to matter, she didn't know. Her fingertips went to the delicate teardrop at her throat. Something about this gift had broken down the last wall she'd erected to keep Ian out. Suddenly, she wanted to let him in.

"Ready?" he asked, his hand on the door lever.

She nodded.

He grasped her hand, and they stepped out of the car.

She supposed she should have expected the photographers, given that the Thunder players were attending as well, but the flashes of light caught her off guard.

Sensing her distress, Ian tightened his hold and pulled her against him, wrapping a protective arm around her waist as he led her inside.

*   *   *

Hours into the event, Ian couldn't wait to get Riley home, peel the dress off her body, and explore her inch by inch, first with his hands, then with his mouth. She was easily the sexiest woman here, not to mention the classiest. Her one-shoulder dress, black with silver trim, slit up one side, revealed an elegant expanse of tanned leg and an incredibly hot, ridiculously high-heeled shoe. His mouth watered, and his cock hardened and approved.

Knowing he had to remain at least through the speech portion of the evening, he'd settle for having a few minutes with her alone. His family had been monopolizing her time ever since they'd arrived. Since they were in public, he'd suffered through each of his brothers dancing with and probably grilling her, but she'd laughed and smiled and obviously enjoyed.

He bit back his jealousy over other men touching her; they were his brothers, after all. He'd settle for killing them over a Sunday basketball game with well-placed elbow jabs and points scored. He wasn't any more pleased with Olivia, her plunging neckline, and clear attempts to make Dylan Rhodes jealous by dancing with other men while eying him to make sure he was watching. At least Avery seemed to be behaving herself…so far.

Even his mother seemed to be enjoying herself, dancing with one man in particular all evening. That was something he intended to question more thoroughly. In fact, he made it a point to interrupt both of his sisters and at least find out what they were up to.

With Riley occupied by Tyler, Ian headed onto the dance floor, where his mother and a silver-haired gentleman were dancing and had been for quite some time.

"Mind if I cut in?" Ian asked.

"Michael, this is my son, Ian. Ian, this is Michael Brooks. His insurance company is a big donor for tonight's auction."

Ian nodded.

The other man extended his hand, and Ian took it. "I've been hearing about you all evening. Your mother is your biggest fan. And I'm impressed with all you've done for the team during your tenure."

"Thank you." Ian hoped the other man wasn't trying to impress him for his mother's sake. He hated suck-ups.

"Unfortunately, I'm a Breakers fan," Michael said with humor and honesty.

"That's a damn shame." So much for his concerns, Ian thought, admiring the man's truthfulness even if his taste in football teams sucked. "And my mother's dancing with you anyway? I'm surprised."

"I've won her over with my charm," Michael said. "She's a lovely lady. Well worth the effort."

"I agree."

"I'll let you have some time together. I'll wait for you at the bar, Emma."

His mother smiled. "I'll see you soon."

"Nice to meet you, Ian." Michael tipped his head and walked away.

His mother followed the other man with her gaze.

"Have you met him before tonight?" Ian asked her.

"We're both on the Juvenile Diabetes Board that planned tonight's event," she said.

Ian pulled her into his arms, and they swayed in time to the slow music. "I'll look into him," he told her.

"You will not. I'm a big girl and—"

"What the hell are they doing here?" Ian asked, interrupting her as he caught sight of his father and Alex walking into the ballroom. Savannah was beside them.

"Who?" His mother glanced toward the entrance.

"My father, his wife, and Alex," Ian said, any peace he'd been feeling this evening evaporating at the sight of them.

Ian had stopped dancing, but his mother pulled him back into their earlier positions. "Don't let them rattle you or interrupt your evening," she said firmly.

He acquiesced to her demands and forced himself to both relax and continue their dance. "I don't understand how you do it."

"How I do what, exactly?" his mother asked.

"Get past what Dad did? Go forward as if nothing happened?"

He met his mother's gaze but saw no stress there, only understanding.

"Your father and I weren't a love match, Ian. You know that already."

"Is that an excuse?" he asked, hearing his bitter tone but unable to stop it.

"No, but it is a fact. The truth is, I was in love before I ever met your father. His name was Jonathan Daniels. He mowed our lawn," she said, blushing.

Ian immediately realized where this conversation was going. "Mom—"

"No. You're going to listen. You're old enough to deal with it, so deal."

He blinked and nodded, knowing when his mother used *that* tone he had no choice but to listen. Besides, she held him captive on the dance floor.

She had his ear, and nobody else could hear. "I'm listening."

"We fell in love, but you know the world I lived in. Your grandparents would never have let me be with him, so we snuck around. Then my father was diagnosed with leukemia. He was terminal and needed someone to take over his hotels. My father and your father's father had been friendly competitors for years. They agreed to merge their businesses and groom Robert to ultimately run both. Our marriage was a part of that deal."

Ian winced at the cold bargain two men had struck at the expense of their children. Of course, Robert had benefited greatly from the merger. He'd become a hotel magnate.

"Did you ever think to say no?" Ian asked.

She shook her head, her eyes filled with unshed tears. "I loved my father very much, and he was dying. He didn't have a son, and I wasn't the kind of woman to take over and run a business."

Her heartfelt sigh broke Ian's heart.

"I had to let Jonathan go."

Ian swallowed hard. To him, it was unimaginable. Could he let Riley go?

Damn, he was in so deep with her he didn't know how he'd ever get out.

"Do you know what happened to him?" Ian asked his mother.

"We agreed it was better if we said good-bye for good."

"So you gave up the man you loved to marry Robert Dare, and he betrayed you." Ian shook his head, his father's behavior suddenly that much more reprehensible in light of what his mother had given up.

She sighed. "Your father and I had what I thought was a traditional marriage, much like many in our social circles. He was away often, and if he cheated on me, I didn't want to know. But when he came to us about Sienna's illness and revealed a whole other family?" She shook her head. "I think I was numb. I stayed that way for years. The only light, the only feelings I let in were for you and your brothers and sisters."

"God, Mom."

"Life isn't always fair. We both know that. But I got five beautiful children out of the deal. I can live with myself because I was faithful. His behavior is on him. I just wish I could have protected you from the pain. And I hate that you're still so angry and you expect the world to let you down."

He tightened his grip on her hand as he led her around the dance floor. "I idolized him. I had him on a pedestal so high..." He shook his head, hating the memories.

"Your father was—is—just a man. And a flawed one, at that. But he loved Savannah, and he hasn't, to my knowledge, cheated on her. Which tells me we were both at fault for agreeing to a loveless marriage to begin with."

He blinked. "You made the same commitment. You were already in love with someone else, and you didn't cheat on him. There's no way to justify it."

"I agree. I'm just saying, people have faults. You have to find a way to accept them and move on. You haven't. And it's eating away at you every single day."

He couldn't argue that point.

"And Sienna's illness wasn't something I'd wish on anyone, especially an innocent child," his mother went on.

Ian nodded. "I haven't exactly been fair to her. Or the rest of them," he admitted, embarrassed in light of his mother's forgiving nature.

"At least you realize it."

"It's too late." Alex had made that clear when none of them had showed up at his invitation.

His mother shook her head. "It's never too late while you're all still here. So let the past go," she said, her words hitting him with deadly accuracy and devastating impact.

Ian inclined his head. He didn't know if he could, but with everything his mother revealed, and for all she'd given up, he promised himself that, for her sake, he'd try.

*　　*　　*

Riley listened to Olivia and Avery's banter, once again enjoying the dynamic between the sisters. She'd already met Ian's mother and instantly warmed to the charming woman who'd gone out of her way to make Riley feel welcomed. She knew Ian appreciated his family in a way many people did not, and as a man who carried hurts from the past, she was grateful he had these three women in his life.

His brothers, who she'd also spent time with, were very much like Alex, when he was in a good mood. They liked toying with their older brother, and by dancing too close with Riley, they knew they were poking at Ian's main weakness. She'd tried to pull away, but they'd laughed and kept her dancing.

"So tell me how you put up with my brother's bossy ways," Avery said, bringing Riley into their conversation.

Since Ian had cut into each sister's dances with other men, and he'd done the same with their mother, they had good reason to ask Riley about Ian's control issues.

Still, Riley couldn't help but blush, knowing there were plenty of times she liked Ian's brand of control. Yet there were many instances when she didn't.

"I suppose I just put him in his place," she said to Avery. She took a sip of her champagne and shrugged, not knowing what else to say.

"And he accepts that?" Olivia asked.

Riley shook her head and laughed. "Not always."

"What happens then?" This, from Olivia.

"I'm not telling." Riley grinned, and the other women merely groaned.

"Good evening, ladies."

Riley stilled at the unexpected sound of Alex's voice. She turned to him, surprised. "What are you doing here?"

He looked handsome in his tuxedo, his shaggy, brown hair giving him even more appeal. She was happy to see him, just not here. Ian would be upset, and that was the last thing she wanted on a night that had otherwise been wonderful so far.

"My parents are big supporters of the cause. Why wouldn't I be here?" He turned toward the other women. "Olivia, Avery. Good to see you," he said.

They each eyed him warily.

Olivia, who Riley had learned was the more outspoken of the two women, straightened her shoulders. "You owe us all an apology," she told him. "Unless you think not showing up when you're invited and have accepted a dinner invitation is the polite thing to do." She raised an imperious eyebrow as she stood up for her brother.

Alex straightened his shoulders. "I think that's between me and Ian."

"Not when I extended the actual invitation on his behalf," Olivia reminded him.

Riley winced. She deliberately stayed out of the conversation. Although the subject upset her, she recognized it was none of her business.

Alex met her gaze and slowly nodded. "You're right. It was rude, and I'm sorry."

Riley blinked in surprise, proud of her best friend for owning his behavior.

"Any chance you'll tell Ian that?" Olivia asked, pushing her luck.

"Tell Ian what?" the subject of conversation asked, joining them.

Riley sighed.

Ian slipped in beside her, wrapping an arm around her and pulling her tightly against him. She automatically leaned into his warmth, savoring the delicious and arousing smell of his cologne. His fingers gripped her waist possessively.

The half siblings and siblings studied each other warily.

"I think Avery and I are going to dance." Olivia spoke first. "It's the first time this DJ is picking up the beat. I don't want to miss out," she said, grasping her sister's hand and pulling her away.

Left alone with the two men, Riley looked to each, wondering who'd break the tension first.

"Alex," Ian said, extending his hand for a shake.

Riley knew what the gesture had cost Ian's pride. She immediately knew he'd done it for her, and her heart filled with love for this enigmatic, self-contained man.

Love.

Oh God.

She didn't have time to analyze the emotion because Alex hadn't answered. Beside her, Ian stiffened at the insult, and they both waited.

"Ian." Alex pumped Ian's hand.

Riley's knees went weak, and she was grateful for Ian's bodily support.

She expected them to find a reason to part ways, but to her surprise, they made small talk about the draft and the potential of both teams during the upcoming season.

A start, she thought, relieved and pleased beyond words. These two men were so important to her she couldn't bear it if they couldn't even make small inroads in their relationship.

"Feeling better?" Alex asked Riley, interrupting her internal musings.

"I'm fine," she answered quickly, shooting him a warning look. She hoped he understood that she wanted him to end this conversation now and not bring up last night's phone call.

"I set a PI on your dad. I should know what that bastard has been up to soon enough." Clearly he'd missed her pointed glance.

"What's going on?" Ian asked.

Riley groaned. "I..." She trailed off, unsure of where to begin.

Alex's gaze shot to hers, his expression apologetic. "I'm sorry, Ri. I just assumed you'd told him."

"Told me what?" Ian asked, his grip on her waist tightening.

"Ouch," she muttered.

He immediately loosened his hold. "What am I missing?" he asked.

She swallowed hard and glanced up at him. "Do you remember earlier, in the limo, I said I wanted to talk to you, and we—umm—got distracted?"

Ian nodded, his jaw tight. He hated being in the dark. Hated more that Riley and his half brother shared some sort of secret.

"Well, it was about this."

"I don't know what *this* is," Ian reminded her, hurt and betrayal flooding through him.

Alex shook his head. "Jesus, Riley. Your old man surfaces, I didn't expect you to keep the news locked up tight. He's the guy you're with." He gestured toward Ian. "Hell, you practically threatened me that I'd lose you if I didn't come around and find a way to get along with him. I figured he was the first one you'd confided in."

"You thought wrong," Ian informed him. "I don't know what the hell is going on, but I plan to find out," he said, his voice vibrating with anger. "Let's go. We're leaving," he told Riley, his hand still holding her arm.

"The hell you are." Alex stepped into his personal space. "You're not leaving with her while you're so pissed off."

"Alex, it's fine," Riley said.

The other man scowled at Ian. "You don't hurt her, you don't lay a fucking hand on her in anger."

"He wouldn't! Alex, back off. This is my problem, not yours," Riley said, defending him.

Ian clenched his free hand, the one he was itching to shove in his half brother's face.

"Do not tell me how to deal with *my* woman," Ian bit out, wanting Alex to know when it came to Riley, Ian had first dibs. "And if you think she'd be with me if I laid a hand on her, then you don't know her as well as you think you do."

"You're the one who doesn't know her."

Point scored, Ian thought.

Alex stepped back. "Call me in the morning," he said to Riley.

She nodded.

Ian immediately led her across the ballroom toward the exit. She struggled to keep up with him in her high heels, but getting her alone and quickly was his first priority.

"We need to say good bye to your family," she said.

"They'll deal."

"What about the speeches? I thought you wanted to stick around for those?" she asked.

"It's fine. I'm well represented."

"Okay," she said quietly, giving in, which told him she knew he wasn't just upset but that he had good reason to be.

He didn't speak again until they were settled in the back seat of the limousine, the privacy partition raised. "You had a problem, and you went to Alex," he said through a clenched jaw.

She blinked at him. "What? No. It wasn't like that. He called me after...wait. I need to start at the beginning." She pushed away from him, curling into herself close to the car door.

He gave her the space she needed. For now.

You already know it's about my father," she said, not wasting time.

"The father you never speak of."

She inclined her head, looking down, as if ashamed.

He couldn't have that. Didn't want her unable to meet his gaze when she confided in him.

"Riley, look at me."

She raised her head, tears in her beautiful blue eyes.

Shit. He slid closer and cupped her chin in his hand. "Tell me."

She swallowed hard.

He waited until she nodded to release her but didn't give her any space between them.

"What Alex said? About you not touching me in anger? It was...it is a sensitive subject for me. For us." She hesitated, and Ian gave her the time she needed to gather her thoughts. "You see, my father was and still is an abusive son of a bitch."

Ian froze, his entire body stilling. He hadn't seen this coming.

Not at all. "He *hit* you?"

Her shoulders sagged slightly. "When I was younger, my mother took the brunt of it. She made sure he directed his fury at her. Then, when Mom died, I stayed out of his way, and he seemed to calm down a little."

He recalled her telling him she'd been sixteen then. He swallowed back the bile rising in his throat.

"Not long after that, he had his gall bladder removed. My stepmom was his hospital nurse. He was on his best behavior while he was wining and dining her and never showed his real self until after they were married." She fiddled with her hands then drew a deep, shuddering breath. "Melissa, my stepmom, she's one tough lady, and he quickly realized he'd chosen the wrong kind of woman this time."

Ian inclined his head. "You've mentioned her. You said she and Alex were your only family."

She nodded. "I adore her. She was the role model my mother should have been. Don't get me wrong, I loved my mom, and I miss her every day. And I know she protected me, but she didn't stand up for herself. If not for Melissa, would I have learned to value myself? To not put stock in the belittling words I grew up around? I'm not so sure."

His stomach churning, Ian reached for her shaking hands, covering them with his own. "You're strong, Riley. I saw that in you from the first day we met."

She smiled at that. "I like to think so."

"Did he ever hit Melissa?" Ian asked.

She shook her head. "They fought often and loudly but...he just seemed to keep himself in check somehow. I think he knew Melissa would go to the cops."

"Your mom never did?" he asked, but he already knew the answer.

"I begged her, but...no. She wouldn't."

"So what happened?" Because something had tipped the precarious balance. That much was obvious.

"Alcohol happened," Riley said in a disgusted voice. "He was always a heavy drinker, but living with Melissa, suppressing his rage, it got worse. And one night, Melissa was working the late shift. He expected me to have his dinner on the table. Not only didn't I do it, but I talked back and...he slapped me. Hard across the face."

A building fury like he'd never felt before filled Ian, making him want to lash out. But his more rational self understood that anger was the last thing Riley needed to see, and he clamped down on his simmering emotions.

"Whenever you're ready," he said in a gentle voice he barely recognized.

She nodded. "I tried, but I couldn't hide the red mark on my face. The next day, Alex saw, and he went berserk. Part of me was surprised he took it so badly. I mean, in my mind, a slap was nothing compared to what he'd done to my mother, though I hid that from Alex as much as I could. Looking back, I thought I was getting off lightly, but Alex was furious."

"Good for him," Ian muttered.

"He cornered my father. He had his hand around his throat, literally cutting off his air supply. He told my father that if he ever touched me again, he was a dead man."

Ian closed his eyes, grateful to the half sibling he'd never bothered to get to know. The man he was irrationally jealous of.

Riley's harsh laugh recaptured Ian's attention. "My father threatened to go to the cops. Can you imagine the irony? Alex told him to go right ahead. Then he followed up his words with a knee to my father's groin and warned him that was just a preview. He said I was off-limits, and he dragged me out of there."

She shook her head, obviously lost in the memory. "I know my father believed his threats, because at seventeen, Alex was massively huge from working out for football."

"What happened next?" Ian asked.

"I called Melissa at work; she came home immediately. She refused to stay with him after that. Alex stood watch while we packed. Melissa told my father I'd be living with her until I was eighteen and if he had a problem with it, to take her to court. With Alex looming over him, he backed off. That was the last night I saw him or heard from him until I got back from Arizona."

Ian narrowed his gaze. "Which brings us to now."

She nodded. "There have been hang-ups on my home answering machine. I never thought it was my father. Then I returned to work to find out he'd left a message while I was away. He said I owed him. And then Friday night, after I got home from shopping, the phone rang, and the person was breathing into my ear. I hung up, and the phone rang again. I answered it yelling, and it was Alex. He wanted to know what was going on. I said it was nothing. He didn't believe me...so I told him."

"Why didn't you call me? Why didn't you trust me enough to let me in before now?"

He forced himself to remain calm, not to yell or show her just how frustrated and angry he really was. Not now, when he finally realized that if he flipped out in any way, he could very likely lose her for good.

"It wasn't a question of whether or not I trusted you, it was humiliating, admitting I grew up that way. Besides, I'd put him so firmly in my past, I never thought about him, talked about him, or wanted to revisit those days." She glanced away.

Once again, he gently redirected her with a touch of his hand. He wanted them communicating, not shutting each other out.

"Do you think I want to deal with my family history? But it's between us, thanks to Alex. I'm trying with him. Because of you."

If he was going to make that kind of effort, he needed to know she'd reciprocate in kind.

"What do you want me to say? I should have told you, and I didn't."

"Because you have trust issues." And here, he'd thought those issues were all his.

She blinked in surprise. "I suppose I do."

Part of him understood, as he was still working through his own. Another part wanted her to know she belonged to him. That she could come to him with anything, *would* come to him first, and know he'd give her everything she needed.

Him.

No one else.

TWELVE

Ian stood with Riley in his living room, the night sky sparkling with stars visible through the large windows. Her revelations about her childhood had humbled him. She was stronger than he'd given her credit for, her relationship with his half brother something he understood much better now.

But that understanding didn't calm his racing heart. And he couldn't help the irrational fear that Alex would always come first for her. Irrational because she hadn't decided to tell Alex about her father before Ian. The timing of the other man's phone call had dictated that choice. And irrational because his jealousy over what she'd told Alex, and when, was based on the insecurities of the child Ian had been, not the man he was now. At least, that's how he should be viewing things.

His mother had begged him to let the past go. If there was ever a time to do that, it was now. The question was whether he could.

"Ian?" Riley asked in a soft voice.

He turned toward her.

She stood in her bare feet, her hair tumbling over her shoulders, her eyes wide and more vulnerable than he'd ever seen them.

She reached for his arm. "I'm sorry I kept you in the dark."

"I know."

"So you're not angry?"

He shook his head. "No, angry wouldn't be the word I'd use."

"Hurt?" she asked.

"I was." He pulled his tie off and held it in one hand. The desire to drag her into the bedroom and tether her to his headboard was strong.

She bit her lower lip. "And now you're not?"

"Now I understand you better. Which was all I ever wanted. To understand what bound you and Alex beyond basic friendship."

She swallowed hard, the soft lines of her throat moving up and down. "And now that you know?"

He walked over to her. "Now, you and I are going to come to an understanding."

"I don't want to lose you," she said before he could elaborate.

"That's not what I want either." In fact, he wanted her bound to his bed, where he'd know she belonged to him, he thought, winding the tie around one hand.

But then he wouldn't know she was there willingly. Olivia's words came back to him. His sisters and his mother all put up with his over-the-top behavior because they were related. They had to, as Olivia had so kindly pointed out. But she was right. If Ian wanted Riley to trust in him enough to come to him first, he needed to extend that same faith.

That didn't come easily to him at all.

"So what now?" she asked.

Now he proved to her he was worthy of any leap of faith he wanted her to make. "I can handle your friendship with Alex. It's an important part of who you are, and I wouldn't ask you to give that up."

She blinked, her eyes filling with tears. "Thank you."

"But...you either trust me or you don't. You either instinctively come to me first or there is no us. On that, I can't compromise." And he didn't know if she could give in on this point that meant everything to him.

"Done."

He blinked.

She wrapped her arms around his neck and held on tightly, sealing her lips against his. Stunned, he couldn't move. Hell, he wasn't sure he'd even heard her correctly.

She tipped her head and looked into his eyes. "First, last, always, Ian."

He let the tie drop to the floor and released a long, relieved breath.

"Mine," he said, lifting her beneath her arms so she could jump up and wrap her legs around him and hold on as he walked them into the bedroom.

He slid her to the floor by the side of the bed. "Turn around," he said in a gruff voice he barely recognized.

She did as he asked, lifting her hair out of the way. He unzipped the gown, sliding the garment off one shoulder and letting the material pool at her feet. The sexy, strapless bra came next, and he kissed the marks left by the confining material, sliding his tongue over her soft skin, working his way down one vertebra at a time.

She trembled but remained in place as his lips hit the sweet spot at the base of her spine, just above the silken thong that settled between her cheeks. He squeezed each round globe, kissing her there, too, before gliding the panties down her long legs.

He rose and splayed his hand across her stomach, his fingertips dipping downward, toward her sex. "Mine," he said once more before spinning her back to face him.

Her eyes were dilated, her cheeks flushed, and she'd pulled her plump bottom lip between her teeth.

"You make me want," she whispered. "You make me believe."

She didn't need to explain. She did the same thing for him.

Before Riley, he didn't believe in romance, relationships, women, or love. He shuddered at the word that danced around his head, tempting him with something he'd long since thought impossible. Yet she was here, by choice. Not running when she knew exactly how demanding he could be.

He cupped her face with both hands and kissed her, taking his time, stroking her lips with his tongue and reveling in her sweet taste. Not demanding anything she didn't willingly give. Instead, he was kissing her as if they had all the time in the world.

He thought of the tie on the floor of the living room. With one choice word, he could have her splayed before him on the bed, acceding to his every command. Lifting his head, he looked down at her. Blue eyes wide, lips well kissed, her breathing ragged, she waited for him to take the lead.

He traced the line of the chain and diamond drop hanging from her delicate neck, and her nipples puckered at his touch. He could have her on her back, hands gripping the headboard as he fucked her wearing nothing but his necklace.

He could. But that wasn't what he wanted from her.

He shed his jacket then unbuttoned his shirt and dropped it to the floor. She reached out a hesitant hand, placing her palm over his heart. In that instant, he accepted that she owned him. He didn't want to fuck her into submission, he wanted to make love to her. It seemed there were still firsts for him, after all.

With none-too-steady hands, he unbuttoned his pants and slid off his trousers and briefs, ridding himself of those as well. Then he lifted her up and dropped her in the center of the bed, coming down on top of her, his body aligning with hers.

He braced his hands on either side of her head. "I don't want anything between us. I want to feel all of you when I slide inside your slick heat."

Her eyes dilated at his graphic words.

"I'm on the pill, but I never have sex without protection," she said.

He was disappointed, but he understood and reached for the nightstand drawer.

"I meant, I've never had sex without it before."

Her words stopped his forward movement, and he came back to her, resuming his earlier position, his thick cock gliding over her feminine heat.

"I'm safe," she continued. "And I know you wouldn't be asking if you had any doubts about yourself."

"I would never put you at risk."

She nodded. "Then I don't want anything between us either."

He released a long-held breath. She'd given him a gift he didn't take lightly. "I've never not used one before either," he assured her.

"I know, Mr. Always in Control." She grinned, her pretty blue eyes glittering with laughter.

"Minx."

She wound her arms around him. "*Your* minx."

He groaned at her words, raised himself up, settling his erection at her entrance. He watched her expression as he eased inside her by increments, not wanting to miss out on one second of this first time. As her body opened, accepting his thick length, taking him in, wet heat slowly enveloped him.

"Oh, Ian, I *feel* you," she murmured in awe.

"I feel you too, baby." And he hadn't been prepared for the emotions flooding through him.

Oh hell, now he knew why they called it making love, he thought, gliding all the way home. So damned good, he thought, his entire body in sensory overload.

Her body clasped him tight, gripping him and connecting them body, heart, and soul. His heart slammed harder inside his chest, beating out a rapid rhythm, screaming ownership and possession of this woman who'd been different from the very first. He stilled, giving himself a second to catch his breath and calm the fuck down. If there'd been any lingering doubts or question of the depth of feelings she inspired, they were gone with this one act.

Before she questioned him, he collected his thoughts and began to move, gliding in and out of her slick sheath. She bent her knees and raised her hips, encouraging him, giving him more depth for each thrust. He picked up rhythm, and she moaned, arching into him each time he drove harder inside her.

Their bodies already had their own rhythm, but skin to skin, everything was elevated, bigger, more, including her cries of pleasure. Faster, harder. He broke into a sweat, braced his arms, and powered into her.

"Yes. Oh God, right there." She arched again, and he made sure the head of his cock hit the same spot inside her.

"Come, baby. I've got you."

Her body stilled and clenched, and she convulsed around him, crying out with each pump of his cock.

"Ian!" She screamed his name, triggering his own hard, fast release.

He came, spilling himself into her, opening his heart and gutting him at the same time.

*   *   *

Riley woke up because her stomach was grumbling. She rolled to find Ian watching her in amusement, his lips twitching with a grin.

"Something funny?" she asked.

"I like watching you sleep. Listening to you? Not so much."

She punched him in the arm. "You made me leave the party before dinner," she reminded him. "I'm starving. And craving ice cream."

He rolled his eyes and laughed. "Luckily for you, I keep a stocked freezer for the girls. My sisters," he added quickly when she raised her eyebrows in question.

"Feed me?" she asked.

He leaned over and kissed her hard on the lips. "Only because you asked so nicely."

He slid out of bed, perfectly comfortable in his nudity, and headed for the kitchen, returning with a large tub of ice cream and one spoon. "Hope you like chocolate swirl."

"Mmm. Works for me." She scooted back in the bed, sitting up as he turned on the bedside lamp and settled in beside her.

"You're not having any?" she asked, holding out her hand for the spoon.

He shook his head and laughed. "We're sharing."

"You're a mean man, making me share my ice cream."

Ignoring her complaint, he popped off the top and placed it on the nightstand before settling in beside her. He dug into the tub and held out the spoon for her to eat.

He fed her, alternating one for him and one for her until they'd had their fill. This was the most relaxed she'd ever seen him, and she understood that something had changed tonight.

Not something, she thought. Everything.

It was as if once she'd verbally committed to him, the walls he'd kept between them had crumbled. Her heart swelled with emotion and the knowledge that somehow she'd captured this man for her own.

The rest of the night continued the same way, with them holed up in his apartment, sharing food, making love, and shutting out the outside world.

Until Sunday morning, when Ian went downstairs and returned with the morning paper. He drank orange juice; she sipped her coffee. She was looking into the back of the sports section that completely covered his face from hers.

"So this is how it's going to be now? You ignoring me for the morning paper? That didn't take long," she joked, reaching for another section of the paper to keep her busy while he read.

"This from the woman who can spend half an hour looking through the apps on her phone?" he asked lightly.

She grinned, still enjoying this lighter, happier Ian.

She flipped through the lifestyle section, pausing at a black-and-white photograph. "It's us!"

The picture had been taken as they exited the limo, Ian obviously holding her protectively. She smiled at the stern expression on his face.

"You're not upset this time?" he asked.

She shook her head. "It's not like everyone doesn't know about us now."

She'd called Alex earlier this morning, as promised, and assured him that Ian wasn't upset, things were good, and he no longer had to worry about her. Ian had been by her side, and she'd chosen her words deliberately, wanting him to know she meant what she'd promised him.

He would come first.

Her cell rang, and she glanced down. "Alex," she murmured.

Ian met her gaze, his expression bland. Whether it was a controlled look or not, she appreciated how hard he was trying.

"I'm sure my sisters will be next once they've seen the paper. They love gossip," he muttered.

She answered the call. "Hi, Alex," she said into the phone.

"I take it you've seen the paper?" he asked.

"We've seen it."

"I hope your father hasn't. The last thing you need is to be a public spectacle, and that's what being with Ian will do for you."

She frowned. "Don't start."

Ian met her gaze with a hard one of his own.

"I have to go. I'll talk to you soon." When she hung up, she forced a smile. "He saw the picture. He's worried it'll provoke my father somehow."

"There's a simple solution for that."

Wary now, she raised her eyebrows. "What would that be?"

"Move in here."

And things had been going so well. Had she expected Ian to change overnight? As long as he was being reasonable and compromising, she reminded herself.

"That's ridiculous. And premature." She'd planned to go home tonight. To take a long bath in her own tub, to play her music, and to gather her thoughts about this intense, emotional weekend.

She rose and walked to the sink to rinse out her coffee cup.

He came up behind her and bracketed his big body around hers, pressing against her, his erection thick against her backside. "I agreed to be reasonable and to back off outside the bedroom, but not when it comes to your safety."

"A couple of heavy-breathing calls and one phone message don't mean I'm not safe."

"You're safer here. With me. And for once, I think Alex would agree with me."

She turned, only to find her front pressed against his. "That may be true, but it doesn't make you two right. He hasn't threatened me."

"Yet."

"I need to go home tonight. We have work Monday, I need to get my clothes, and I already told you I can't be seen coming to work with you in the mornings." She eyed him warily, really hoping he wasn't going to turn this into a fight.

He let out a frustrated groan. "Okay, answer this one question for me, and then we'll decide together. Would you put it past your father to lay a hand on you?"

He had her, and she knew it. She hung her head, her shoulders dropping in defeat. "No."

He braced his hands on her shoulders. "Listen to me. I'm not trying to run your life. I'm not even trying to get you to move in here just because it's what I want."

Her stomach did a flip at the admission.

"I'm doing it for your safety."

"Never mind that you get what you want in the end."

He grinned. "That's just a side benefit. Can you deny that apartment building of yours is too easy to get into?"

"No." She hated that he was right. Not because being here with Ian didn't appeal to her but because it did. She wanted them together for the right reasons, when they were both ready.

Riley had spent too many years on her own, rebuilding her ego and her belief in herself after the time her father had spent tearing her down. Giving into Ian was something she'd prefer happened slowly, at her own comfort level. Instead, her bastard father was forcing her hand.

"Let me drive you back to your place. You can pack your things and follow me back here in your own car. Tomorrow morning, nobody will know where you're arriving from."

She blinked, startled at his concession. "I really thought—"

"I was pushing my own agenda," he finished for her.

She averted her gaze, embarrassed. She figured he'd pulled the danger card and then she'd have no choice but to drive to the stadium with him, allowing him to put his stamp all over her at work.

"I may not have given you any reason to trust me, but I said I'd compromise. And I'm doing it."

She heard the hurt in his tone. "You are. I'm sorry I'm such a bitch," she said.

"As long as you're *my* bitch." He grinned, swatted her on the ass, and walked away, leaving her with her mouth open in surprise.

THIRTEEN

Riley arrived at work on Monday morning to find Dylan wanted them to take a quick trip to Manhattan to check out a city hotel owned by the same company as the place in Phoenix. Forty-eight hours, in and out. She agreed to head home and pack.

She called Ian first, knowing he'd appreciate the gesture. Although he was in a meeting across town, he took her call immediately. He wasn't pleased they'd be apart so soon after she'd moved in, but he didn't ask her not to go or interfere. He couldn't leave the meeting he was in and instead insisted she take a car service to her apartment, charge it to the company, and make sure the driver walked her up to her door and waited for her to return to the car. He didn't want her alone.

She didn't argue, not wanting to add pressure to his day. She already knew how difficult he found it to let her go on these trips, and she understood so much more now, especially since many of his father's business trips had been a cover for time with Savannah and his *other* family.

While away, Riley made sure to call him often, and though her room was full of flowers, Dylan had no complaints about phone calls from Ian.

In other words, Ian was living up to his word. In return, she picked up souvenirs, silly things like a miniature Empire State Building and an *I Love NY* hat just to show Ian she thought of him too.

She arrived home Wednesday morning, heading straight from the airport to work.

Angie greeted her with a smile and her messages.

"You're amazing," Riley told the other woman.

"Thanks! Let me know if you need anything."

"I will."

"Oh! There's a package for you on your desk," Angie added.

"Got it!" Riley said as she entered her office.

She parked her small travel suitcase in the corner and flopped into her chair. "Home sweet home away from home," she muttered, kicking off her shoes beneath her desk.

She might have work to do, but she wanted to see Ian first. Still, the package in brown wrapping called to her. She wondered if he'd bought her something while she was away. She immediately touched the pendant he'd given her. She only removed it to shower then put it back on to sleep.

She wasn't stupid, knew it was ridiculously expensive, but its worth wasn't in its dollar value. For Riley, the necklace was Ian's statement, proof of how well he knew her taste and what she meant to him. She didn't want or need anything else from him, she thought, as she ripped into the package.

Inside was a box and inside that, a picture frame. Had the silly man framed the picture of them from the newspaper? That was something she'd cherish, their first photograph together.

She turned over the rectangular frame, took one look at the picture, and screamed, dropping it onto her desk. "Oh my God!"

"Riley, are you okay?" Angie popped around the doorframe.

"I'm fine," she lied.

The other woman narrowed her gaze. "Are you sure?"

"Yes," she whispered.

Angie left, and Riley turned over the offending picture. Riley's beautiful mother, her face bruised and battered, stared back at her. Obviously an old photo, it was faded and had been crumpled and straightened again to be sent here.

Ian. She had to show Ian. Not because she'd promised him, but because he was the only person she wanted now.

She held the frame against her chest, not wanting anyone else to see, and ran for his office.

His secretary smiled when she saw Riley.

"Is he in?" she asked.

The older woman nodded. "But he's on a call."

Riley didn't care. She passed by the woman's desk and let herself into his office.

He looked up when she burst in, his serious expression transforming into a smile. "I have to go," he said to whomever was on the phone, disconnecting the call.

Ian rose and started toward her, stopping when he caught sight of her pale face and wide, panicked eyes. "What's wrong?"

She shook her head, and he realized she was clutching something close to her heart. He wrapped his hands around hers. "Can I see?"

She released her grip. "It's my mother," she said in a pain-wracked voice.

He looked down at the gruesome reminder of her past pain, and a combination of nausea and rage filled him. "Where did you get this?"

"The package was delivered here," she said, her voice dull.

Ian narrowed his gaze, trying to decide what concerned him more. The delivered photograph or Riley's reaction. "Come sit."

He led her to his leather couch and eased her down, setting the picture facedown on the table in front of them. "Riley?"

"I'm going to kill him," she said, color returning to her cheeks.

Not if Ian got to the son of a bitch first.

"We need to call the police. They need to document what's been happening, okay?"

She nodded. "My mother never did. I want it on record," she said, sounding stronger.

He let out the breath he'd been holding, relieved she seemed to be coming back to herself.

"Have you been home yet?"

She shook her head. "Dylan was coming straight here, so I did too. I wanted to see you."

He smiled at that, touching his forehead to hers. "I'm right here."

"I came straight to you," she said, her gaze on the picture frame. "I opened it up and came right to you."

He gathered her hair and pulled it back, off her face. "You did good. And I'm going to take care of it," he promised her.

She blinked at that, her posture stiffening.

Wrong direction, he thought. She didn't want him fighting her battles or acting like she couldn't take care of herself. He got that about her.

"I missed you," he said, changing the subject.

"Me too. I brought you presents."

His heart warmed at the gesture. "How about we take the day off?" he suggested, needing to be alone with her. He needed to slide deep inside her willing body and know she was safe. And his.

She frowned. "I have summaries to write."

"Did Dylan say he needed or wanted them today or first thing tomorrow?"

She shook her head.

"Then relax. You earned the rest of the day. And I'm the boss. I can do whatever I want."

She rolled her eyes and laughed. "You sure can. But we need to stop at the police station on the way home," she said, her tone growing more serious.

"I'll be right there with you," he promised her.

She grasped his hand and squeezed tightly. "I don't know what he wants from me after all this time."

Ian couldn't imagine. But he intended to find out. Until now, he'd been okay letting Alex handle looking into the son of a bitch, but now that her father had stepped up his game, Ian was getting involved. In deference to Riley's feelings, he'd talk to Alex, but that didn't mean he'd leave things solely in his half brother's hands.

* * *

Ian had not only lived alone, but he'd planned to remain that way. He wanted Riley with him, but he'd expected some internal tension over having her clothes in his closet and drawers, her feminine bottles and things in his bathroom and personal space. To his surprise, they blended seamlessly.

Once she'd returned from New York and made herself at home, spreading out and not keeping to one small space, he found comfort in the things that assured him she was there and real. The problem, in his mind, was that she wasn't there by choice. Her father's implied threats may have forced her to move in with him, but if he had his way, she wouldn't be leaving when the bastard was taken care of.

If left up to the cops, that might be awhile. Their stop at the nearest precinct was, as he'd feared, a waste of time. Short of documenting the phone calls and gift, there was no proof either of those things had been the other man's doing. Though the cop who'd taken Riley's statement had been sympathetic, especially after seeing the picture of her badly beaten mother, he didn't think she had enough evidence to rise to the level needed for an order of protection.

Riley would need to prove she had reasonable cause to believe she was in immediate danger of becoming a victim of domestic violence, and given that she hadn't seen her father in ten years, one phone call that wasn't even a direct threat didn't suffice. The officer couldn't suggest anything more than to remind her to be in touch if she heard from her father or received anything more harassing than the calls she'd received so far.

Riley left defeated, and Ian hated seeing his normally spunky, bright girl feeling so beaten down. He swore to do more than the cops in order to make things right.

He started by arranging for a surprise for later that would put a smile on Riley's face. It would also give him a chance to poke further into the situation and see if there was anything more he could find out about her old man.

*   *   *

Riley awoke from a long nap feeling refreshed and calmer than she'd been earlier today. She stared at the ceiling of Ian's bedroom, the events of the morning coming back to her full force. She closed her eyes, refusing to think about her father at all. If she allowed him any space in her mind, be it fear or anger, she gave him power. And that was the one thing she refused to cede ever again.

Instead, she shifted focus to her location, looking around the beautiful and massively large bedroom, amazed at how much her life had changed in such a short time. From the new job, to the new man in her life, to moving in with Ian, albeit temporarily, nothing was the same as it had been just a few weeks ago. And it wasn't just logistics, career, and Ian that had changed.

She was changing.

Learning to accept things from others, from small items and gifts to larger, more significant offers, like a new job and a place to live, she was slowly bending. Giving up her hard-won and fought-for independence. And the scariest of all, coming to count on having Ian in her life.

But she was also realizing that relying on others didn't make her weak…it made her human. Nor did it escape her notice that Ian was changing too, and that made her own transformation somewhat easier to accept. She couldn't demand he alter who he was to accommodate her and not do the same for him.

She was growing up, she thought with a laugh. Ironic, since before meeting Ian, she'd believed her independence defined her and was the most important thing in her life.

"Something funny?" Ian slid beside her on the bed and pulled her into his arms.

"Not really. Just thinking about how different things are for me lately."

"Good different or bad different?" he asked, nuzzling her neck with his lips.

"Are you searching for compliments?" she asked.

He nipped her collarbone in reply, and she groaned. Every nerve ending tingled, her nipples puckered, her body on high alert, ready for him. Another thing that had changed. She was always sexually charged now.

"Get showered and ready; we're going out for dinner tonight with another couple," he told her.

She bolted up in bed. "What? Who?"

He yanked her down and back into his arms, where she immediately felt safe and secure. "Your stepmother and her husband."

She rolled so she could look at his handsome face. "I don't get it."

"What's not to get? You love her, I haven't met her.... It's time."

"Does my father resurfacing have anything to do with this sudden invitation?" she asked him.

Ian shrugged. "I won't deny it put the idea in my head. Maybe she's heard from him too."

"She would have told me," Riley said.

"Why? Have you told her?" he pointedly asked.

She winced. "Score," she muttered under her breath.

He chuckled and kissed the tip of her nose. "Maybe she doesn't want to worry you, same reason you haven't told her. Or maybe he's only focused on you. We need to know. And she needs to be prepared, just in case."

"You're right."

An arrogant grin edged his mouth. "Say that again."

"No."

He cupped her sex with his big hand, and she arched up, immediately seeking more pressure. She'd shed her skirt when she climbed into bed, and he brushed one finger over her mound, drawing small circles over her clit, causing an exquisite pressure to build inside her.

"Mmm."

"Like that, do you?" he asked, nibbling on her neck at the same time he continued his sensual assault.

"Yes. Harder," she said, eyes half-mast as she focused on the pleasure slowly mounting.

He stopped all movement. "First, say it again. 'Ian, you were right.'"

She opened her eyes wide to find him above her, grinning like a fool. Hmm. Give him the words he sought or suffer orgasm deprivation—because she had no doubt he'd stop completely. Controlling bastard, she thought, not really meaning it. Not anymore.

"Ian, you're right," she said, and he came down on top of her and spent the next thirty minutes catering to her body, giving her two orgasms that had her screaming out her release.

Then he plunged deep inside her, whispering *mine* in her ear and taking her to heights she'd only dreamed of before he'd come barging into her life.

*   *   *

Riley drove to work the next morning, on a high from how well Ian and her stepmom had gotten along. Ian had charmed Melissa and had a long after-dinner drink with her husband, David, while Melissa gushed over the new man in Riley's life. In her mind, Ian was the perfect catch, and she heartily approved. With her husband being a Thunder fan, the two men had had plenty to talk about.

The only downside to the night, in Ian's mind, was that not only had Melissa not heard from Douglas Taylor, she'd offered him no new insight into why he'd suddenly started harassing Riley.

For Riley, however, this was good news. The best, really. It meant that, in all likelihood, she didn't have to worry about her father going after Melissa, and now that both she and David were aware of the possibility, they could take steps to protect her, just in case.

That Ian had invited Melissa over spoke volumes about his unspoken feelings for her, Riley thought. Although she knew she loved him, she'd remained silent on the subject. She might be changing, but she was old-fashioned at heart, and she wanted, needed him to say it first.

Mine, while possessive and arousing, wasn't the same thing. She needed the words. In her mind, saying them was the ultimate vulnerability. For as much as he'd given her, as much as he was learning to compromise—and laugh—as much as she believed in his feelings for her, him saying those three little words would be the ultimate gift. The final breakdown in that wall they'd each erected to protect their hearts.

Once in her office, she settled in to work, and the morning passed quickly.

Her phone rang, and she assumed it was either Dylan or Ian, ready to go out for lunch, and she answered on the first ring. "Riley Taylor."

"You're not a big shot to me," a familiar voice from her past said.

Her blood ran cold, and she sat up straighter in her seat. "What do you want?" she asked the man she'd hoped to never hear from again.

"To tell you that you don't impress me. You're just playing dress up, little girl. I know you're not worth a damn. You never have been. And now that you're with that hotshot, I have leverage."

"I don't know what you mean," she said, gripping the phone so hard her fingers ached.

"I mean, I don't have to worry about your football player and his threats anymore. Even if he manages to find me, I can do plenty of damage to your new boyfriend's reputation before he does."

So Alex was right when he'd worried about those photographs with Ian. Nausea filled her, and she fought the swirling sensation in her stomach.

"Leave him alone. In fact, go back into whatever hole you crawled out of."

"Then do something for me."

She began to shake. "What do you want?"

"Money. Thanks to you, I lost my wife, my house, I have nothing left, and I've just been waiting for the right time to collect."

"I don't have any money," she said, her throat dry.

Her father let out a mean laugh she remembered from her childhood, from the times she'd curl in a ball while he used it on her mother. Before he slapped her around.

"The whole city knows how much money your boyfriend's got. You make sure I get my share, and I won't show up everywhere he goes and make a scene."

"Ian won't care," she whispered, hoping she was right.

"But you do. You never liked to be the center of attention. Never liked it when people looked at you. Because you're trash, and everyone knew it."

"Because I had an alcoholic father who beat the crap out of my mother," she shouted at him.

"Don't blame me for your failings. I'll be in touch by the end of the day. Get me money, or I'll call the news and create enough scandal for Ian Dare to drop you like the trash you always were."

Tears leaked from her eyes. "What did I ever do to make you hate me so much?" she asked, but he'd already hung up.

She slammed the phone down, missing the cradle. So she banged it again and again, sobs wracking her body. By the time she pulled herself together, her head pounded, and she was sure she looked like roadkill. She grabbed her compact mirror and fixed herself as best she could, not wanting to alert anyone at work to her personal problems.

Her father wanted money, she thought. The one thing she didn't have. The two men in her life both did, but she discounted going to each, for very different reasons.

Alex was out for two reasons. The first being she'd promised Ian she'd always go to him first, and she meant to keep that promise. The second being that Alex would find her father and beat him within an inch of his life. As appealing as that thought was—and Riley refused to dwell on what kind of person that made her—she couldn't allow him to ruin his career and his life over her. He'd done enough for her over the years, and she wouldn't repay his friendship and love by knowingly destroying him.

Which left Ian. Without a doubt, she knew he'd react the same way as Alex, and she wouldn't put him in that position either. Both men had too much at stake professionally, both were public figures, and both deserved more than to lose everything because her father had tripped their anger.

In her heart, she didn't believe Ian would care if her father did his best to humiliate him in public, but Riley would. She also couldn't subject his family—his mother and sisters especially—to her father's hostility and venom. They didn't deserve the fallout sure to come from Ian being associated with Riley.

God, she hated the man. He was forcing her to lie to Ian, the one thing she didn't want to do. She mentally replayed her conversation with Ian. *"You either trust me or you don't. You either instinctively come to me first or there is no us. On that, I can't compromise."*

She honed in on the word 'first.' She promised would come to him *first*, which implied she'd go to him over Alex. She was parsing, she knew. Playing word games to justify not telling him about her father's call and threats. Word games were all she had.

She couldn't go to him about this, not because she didn't trust him, but because she did. She trusted him to take care of things, to either kill her father or agree to pay him off. She couldn't allow the former, and the latter? She shook her head. She might be learning to accept things from him, but this was out of the question. Her father would only keep coming back for more, over and over again. He'd never be out of their lives. She shuddered at that.

Somehow, Riley needed to handle her father herself. No matter how scared she was, and her stomach cramped with pain at the thought, she needed to handle him alone.

She played with the necklace dangling against her chest, finding small comfort as she touched the pendant, and thought about how to proceed.

What to do.

The idea, when it came to her, was simple. It also devastated her. But most important, it would buy her time and protect Ian and his family from her father until she could figure out a more permanent solution.

FOURTEEN

Ian's stomach grumbled.

He glanced at his computer screen, his gaze on Riley's instant message window that he kept up and available to him at a moment's notice. He thought of the day he'd taken her in his office, and his cock hardened immediately. Sex or food, he thought wryly.

Ian: Hungry?

She didn't answer immediately, so he gave her some time to return to her desk.

He called the private investigator he'd put on Riley's father and left the man another voice mail. Ian understood it took time to compile information, but dammit, he wanted answers now.

A few minutes later, with no word from Riley, he decided to go find her. He'd had lunch with her all week, and though they hadn't explicitly discussed today, she'd have let him know if she had a meeting.

He walked through the offices, which were mostly empty, as it was lunchtime, and stepped into her private domain. She wasn't around. He figured he'd leave her a note and go grab something in the cafeteria. Maybe she'd come find him and they could share a quickie for dessert. At her desk, he looked around for a piece of paper, his gaze immediately coming to rest on a notepad.

Cash-In Pawn Shop was scrawled in her handwriting.

Ian narrowed his gaze. What the hell would she need to hock and why?

Her father.

Ian didn't know what was going on, but he'd bet his life it had something to do with that bastard.

He pulled out his phone and saw missed calls from earlier that morning. His half brother had called twice. No message.

Shit.

He hit redial, and Alex answered on the first ring.

"You're a hard man to get a hold of," Alex said.

Ian scowled. He'd have to get his phone checked. "What do you want?"

"I have the report on Riley's father. I thought I'd share."

Ian narrowed his gaze at his half sibling's unexpected overture. "Go ahead."

"Douglas Taylor has been living on the streets for the last two years. He lost his job and then his house to the bank when the market crashed a few years back. He's flat broke and an alcoholic, to boot. Occasionally he sobers up and gets a job washing dishes, but then he has money for booze, so the cycle starts up all over again."

The words *flat broke* reverberated in Ian's brain. "Riley left the name of a pawnshop downtown scrawled on her desk."

"Son of a bitch," Alex said.

"That bastard's been in touch again. He probably wants money," Ian said.

"But she doesn't have anything of value to sell," Alex said.

Ian thought of the necklace he'd bought her, and the pain of betrayal nearly gutted him. "Yeah. She does."

And she'd chosen that route instead of trusting him. He shook his head, unable to believe it.

"What's the address of the pawnshop? I'll meet you there," Alex said, breaking into Ian's thoughts.

He shared the address on the paper and disconnected the call.

* * *

Riley pulled up to the pawnshop in a really horrible part of town. Luckily, she got a parking spot out front. She shouldn't be here long, which was a relief, considering the neighborhood gave her the creeps. A man with a cup sat on the ground beside the shop with a sign asking for money. And a gang of kids wearing matching colors hung out across the street.

She shivered and quickly walked inside. The shop was dimly lit, the linoleum on the floor filthy and cracked. There were other people in the store, lingering at the counter and haggling with an older woman near the back.

A middle-aged man greeted her. "What can I do for you?" he asked.

She still wore the necklace, unwilling to take it off until the last possible second. She reached for it, as she'd been doing since she'd made the decision to sell it to pay off her father.

The weight of it gave her comfort, making her feel like she had Ian beside her. From it, she drew strength. "I umm…"

"I ain't got all day, lady. You selling that piece or not?"

"I need a minute," she snapped and turned away from the counter.

He mumbled about indecisive women and turned to help another customer.

She ran her hand over the cool diamond, memories of Ian bombarding her. The vulnerability in his face when he'd asked her to accept the gift, the relief when she had. His placing the pendant around her neck and his huskily spoken words, *It's perfect. Just like you.*

She clasped the beloved piece tighter, knowing she couldn't do it. She couldn't part with something Ian had given her, and she wouldn't cave in to her father. He'd bullied her throughout her childhood, and she was finished.

Done.

It had taken her coming here to see what a foolish mistake she might have made. Ian would know the necklace was missing, and she couldn't lie to him. She'd promised him she would come to him first and always, and that's what she would do.

"Thanks anyway," she called out to the man, walking at a fast pace out the front door. She reached the sidewalk and breathed in the stuffy, humid air, wanting nothing more than to get into her air-conditioned car.

"Riley."

She turned to see her father climb out of the passenger seat of a beat-up car that sat behind hers.

"Long time no see."

Her skin crawled at the sound of the voice that had haunted her nightmares for years. He didn't look well. His skin was sallow, his body so thin and gaunt his clothes hung on his narrow frame. Dark circles were heavy beneath his eyes, and red splotches stained his cheeks.

"What are you doing here?" she asked.

"I've been keeping an eye on you. Imagine my surprise when you left your cushy job and drove here. I guess I can still get you to do what I say." He gestured toward the pawnshop behind her.

"You're following me?" Revulsion filled her. "But you can't get into the stadium without permission."

"Don't be an idiot. I waited until you pulled out of the lot."

She folded her arms across her chest. "Well, I don't have anything for you right now," she said and started for her car.

He lunged, grabbing her and dragging her into an alley beside the store.

He backed her into the wall, giving her nowhere to go. The overwhelming stench of alcohol and body odor hit her hard.

"Let's start over." He grabbed her arm so hard she knew she'd have bruises. "We agreed you'd get me money."

"We didn't agree on when," she gritted out.

He shook her hard. His fingers bit into her skin, his frail appearance belying his strength. "Where's the cash?"

"There isn't any. Go ask the guy in the shop if you don't believe me."

He snatched her purse from her shoulder, nearly wrenching her arm from its socket. Opening it, he began tossing her things onto the ground in a mad search for cash. When he came to her wallet, he shoved her bag at her, and she held it tightly while he looked through her wallet. Good luck, she thought. If she had twenty dollars in there, it was a lot.

He pocketed the small amount of money he found and threw her wallet to the ground. "Where is it? In your pockets?"

"I said didn't sell anything," she said coldly.

"Bitch." He slapped her hard across the face, her head smacking the wall with the force of the hit.

She saw stars, the pain overwhelming and intense.

"Why are you here? What were you planning to sell?" he asked at the same time his gaze focused on her chest. "This is it, right?" He put his hands on her beloved necklace. "Your boyfriend buy this for you?"

She closed her eyes, unable to stand being this close to him and unable to believe she'd ever considered selling something so precious to her.

That's when her fight instinct kicked in, and she kneed him in the groin hard. She didn't have enough leverage to take him down, but the element of surprise along with the initial pain had him rearing back in shock.

"You stupid bitch."

She expected him to slap her again and braced, ready to duck, but he grabbed for the necklace instead and yanked hard, breaking the chain.

He held up his prize. "This oughta net me a nice sum. Don't think I'm done with you either." He turned and headed out of the alley and back onto the street.

"Oh hell no," she muttered, having had enough. Not just for today but for a lifetime.

She started after him and slammed into him with the full force of her body, taking him down. He rolled, flipping over, and she ended up on top of him, her hands around his throat, and she began to squeeze...

Her mother's face flashed in front of her eyes, and she tightened her grip. "I hate you," she screamed at him as his body bucked and he clawed at her in an attempt to dislodge her.

"Riley!"

She heard her name at the same time sirens sounded. Hands gripped her by the shoulders, pulling her off him, but she was too hysterical to focus on who'd come to her rescue or what had happened to the man who'd never been a real father.

*   *   *

Ian pulled up to the pawnshop just after Alex. It took mere seconds for him to process the scene. Riley's hands around a man's throat, Alex pulling at her shoulders. Her father began to rise, coughing and sputtering but clearly intending to run. Ian slammed the man back to the ground just as a police car screeched to a halt, and the cop approached the scene.

"She attacked me," her father sputtered at the uniformed cop.

The coward, Ian thought.

"Shut the hell up." Ian shoved his foot on her father's chest so he couldn't move until a cop showed up and took over.

The officer pulled the older man to his feet. Before he could ask questions, a middle-aged man walked out of the pawnshop and headed for the cop.

"He attacked her in the street," the shop owner said, gesturing to Riley's father.

"You're the one who called it in?" the cop asked.

The other man nodded.

With a grim expression, the cop pulled her father's hands behind his back and cuffed him while reading him his rights. Then he turned to the guy from the store. "Wait here. We'll need to take your statement."

With her father subdued, Ian turned to focus on Riley. He saw her on the ground, Alex holding her in his arms.

He gritted his teeth and walked over to them. "She okay?" he asked.

Alex met his gaze, a warning look in the other man's eyes.

Right. Like Ian was going to start a fight with her now. Thanks for the faith, he thought with disgust.

One of the cops came up beside Ian.

"Ri?" Alex eased her away from him. "The police are here."

"Does this belong to you?" The cop held out the necklace Ian had given her. "He had it clutched in his hand."

She nodded then groaned and grabbed her head. "Yes," she said, not meeting Ian's gaze.

"It's evidence for now, but you'll get it back when the case is over. Did you hit your head?" the officer asked.

"He slapped me, and I slammed into the wall in the alley," Riley said, her voice hoarse from screaming.

Ian winced and wished he'd done more than restrained the son of a bitch for the police.

"An ambulance is on its way. You're going to need to be checked for a concussion."

"But—"

"No arguing," Alex said, helping her rise to her feet.

She raised her tear-stained face to Ian's for the first time. "Stay with me?" she asked him.

He couldn't say no.

Didn't want to.

But the pain over her putting herself through this when she could have turned to him devastated him. He'd asked her for one thing if they were going to go forward, and at the most crucial moment, she hadn't kept her promise.

An hour later, he and Alex sat in the hospital waiting room while Riley was taken in for tests.

"You'll take her home from here?" Alex asked, breaking the uncomfortable silence.

Ian shifted in his seat. "Actually I was going to ask you to do it."

The other man narrowed his gaze. "I don't get it."

Ian studied his hands, trying to figure out how to explain his most personal feelings to a guy he barely knew. "After the fundraiser, I thought Riley and I had come to an understanding."

You either trust me or you don't. You either instinctively come to me first or there is no us. On that, I can't compromise, he'd told her.

"Yet at the first sign of trouble, she went off on her own," Ian said.

Alex shrugged. "Told you from the get-go she was independent."

"Yeah. But I thought we were working on how to compromise. Hell, I compromised on you," Ian said, because he knew the other man could take it.

Alex burst out laughing. "I hear you. The thing is, you just saw firsthand why she doesn't trust. She didn't call me either."

Ian nodded. He'd give her that. That might have sent him completely over the edge.

"I'm still not sure we can go forward from here." And that was about all he wanted to say on the subject to his half brother. "I just need to know you'll be there for her." Because he knew she shouldn't be alone.

It would kill him to leave her, but he had no choice. He'd made his needs clear—and he didn't think he was being unreasonable. He'd done everything he could to give her the space she needed to be independent, backing off from his possessiveness at work, not pushing on the unsafe apartment issue…well, not much.

Yet when the ultimate shit came down, she'd gone it alone.

"I'll be here," Alex said. "I always am."

Ian nodded. He knew better than to thank the other man.

So he'd wait for news she was okay. Then he'd leave, ripping out his heart…along with hers. Because after her choices, what kind of partnership did they have? He might not be an expert on relationships, but he knew for sure without trust, they had nothing.

* * *

Riley had a concussion and mild bruising. The doctor told her she could go home as long as someone was there to make sure to check her every hour. He also advised her to watch for more severe symptoms—headache getting worse, vomiting, and extreme dizziness. Since she knew Ian wouldn't let her out of his sight, she promised the doctor she'd follow his instructions. He left her to inform Ian and Alex of her condition and to send them in to see her.

She lay with her eyes closed, her head pounding, moving only when she heard the rustling of the curtain in her small cubicle. She opened her eyes in time to see Alex enter, and she immediately looked beyond him for Ian.

He wasn't there.

"Where's Ian?"

Alex settled into a chair beside the makeshift bed. "I'm sorry…he left."

"Work emergency? Or is he that mad at me?" she asked.

Alex groaned. "I've seen him angry, and I wouldn't say that now. He's…hurt. Really hurt. What the hell were you thinking?"

"My father wanted cash. I was thinking that I'd pawn the necklace and buy myself some time to figure out what to do. Otherwise, he threatened to show up at places like the fundraiser and embarrass Ian. I didn't want to put him or his family through that."

He shook his head. "That's bullshit."

She raised her gaze. "Excuse me?"

"You heard me. You ran scared. The man told you to come to him with *anything*, and the first chance you had to do that, you took off on your own. To pawn the necklace he gave you to pay that lowlife son of a bitch."

"I didn't go through with it!" she said, raising her voice.

"That's not the point!" he shouted back. "That moron I call a half brother is the best thing that ever happened to you, and you lost him, and why? Because you're afraid to trust, that's why. Everything has to be on your terms. You won't accept help from the people who love you, including me. I know how that makes me feel, so I can only imagine how Ian's suffering."

Tears filled her eyes. "You're taking his side?"

He grasped her hand. "I'm taking your side, Ri. Always. And I know that you love him."

She blinked. "I never said that."

"You didn't have to." He shook his head, his expression thoughtful. "Honest to God, if you had to fall for a guy, why did it have to be him?"

She managed a smile. "I don't see how it matters. He's gone."

"Only because you won't give him what he needs. Look, I'm the last guy to talk about relationships, but even I can see he's changed for you. So why can't you do the same thing for him?"

She glanced down. "I'm scared," she whispered. "What if I rely on him and he's not there?"

"Listen to me. Kids are born, and they're supposed to know their parents will be there for them, to keep them safe, to love them. You never had that, so you learned early to count on you. Then later, you found it in yourself to trust me."

She swallowed, and it physically hurt. "Because you were always by my side."

"I don't see Ian going anywhere if you open yourself up to him."

"I told him I would…and I didn't."

"Can you? In the future?"

Riley searched her heart. She wanted to. She did…but she just didn't know, if pushed again, if she'd turn inward like she always did.

"Ms. Taylor?" A woman dressed in a skirt and blouse, her blonde hair pulled back in a ponytail, walked into the room. "I'm Madison Evans, but you can call me Madison. I'm a social worker."

Riley's head whipped up. "I don't need—"

"Good to meet you," Alex said, rising from his chair, nearly stumbling over his feet in an effort to say hello. "I'm Alex Dare, a friend of Riley's."

The pretty woman appeared to be about Riley's age. She smiled and shook his hand, no sense of recognition in her expression.

"Nice to meet you too," she said, dismissing him by turning back to Riley.

Alex's mouth opened in disbelief.

Riley did her best not to laugh. Poor Alex wasn't used to not being fawned over by women.

"I appreciate you coming by, but honestly, I don't need a social worker," Riley told the woman.

"Don't listen to her. She protests too much. Finish what you were going to say." Alex shot Riley a pointed look.

Madison glanced back and forth between them before again focusing on Riley. "I was just going to tell you that I speak to all domestic abuse victims who come through the hospital."

Riley wrinkled her nose. "But I'm not—"

"You are." Alex came to stand by her side, placing a calming hand on her shoulder.

Madison stepped closer to the bed. "The reports say you were injured when you were attacked by your father?" she asked gently.

Riley met her gaze. "Yes."

"If you'd like to set up an appointment for counseling, it might help to talk to someone."

"It definitely might," Alex said.

"I get the point." Riley accepted the woman's business card, doubtful she'd be using it. "Thank you."

"That's my job, and I'm good at it, if you don't mind me saying so. I'd like the chance to help you work through whatever issues might have arisen from this experience."

Riley nodded. "Okay."

Madison smiled. "Okay."

She strode out of the room, Alex's stare never leaving her retreating form.

Riley narrowed her gaze, but she had no chance to ask about his obvious interest in a woman who looked nothing like his usual bimbo type.

"She's right," Alex immediately said.

"You think I need help." Riley glanced down at the blanket covering her.

"I don't think talking can hurt."

"Look at you, being all diplomatic." She pursed her lips and studied the woman's card in her hand.

"I just want you to be happy, and you were happy with Ian. He was good for you."

Riley grinned. "Don't sound like you're choking on those words."

Alex laughed. "Give me a break. I called him with information on your father, and I thought that was being generous. Now I'm singing his praises." He shook his head. "I'm not sure how much more I can handle in one day."

"Alex?"

"Yeah?"

"What if Ian's gone for good?" She voiced her biggest fear. "He doesn't let people in easily either. What if I pushed him so far he'll never come back?"

"Then he's the idiot I always thought he was."

"You're so bad," she said, laughing through her tears.

"And you're so good. Get the help you need. It's important for you, whether or not Ian is in your life."

FIFTEEN

A few days after the incident with her father, Riley left the comfort of Alex's house and headed home to her apartment. On doctor's orders, she'd taken the rest of the week off from work and used the time to rest and heal, and to think.

Her mother had been gone well over a decade. Riley had been out of her father's house for ten years. All this time, she thought she had survived her past unscathed. She looked at the box of her things Ian had sent over, and her eyes filled with tears. Apparently she hadn't emerged as unscathed as she thought.

She glanced at the clock. Melissa would be here soon, and Alex was coming to take her for dinner. Not only were they the extent of her family, they were the extent of her friends too. She'd been kidding herself thinking that the co-workers she used to have an after-work drink with were real friends. She didn't let anyone close enough to have any *friends*.

She ducked her head, only now accepting that she had trust issues that just might rival Ian's. Except he'd been making an effort to change, up until the point when he'd abandoned her at the hospital. Of course, she knew the obvious reasons for his disappearance from her life. She'd disappointed him by handling things with her father herself and not turning to him like she'd promised. She also knew his bailing on her had to do with his insecurities, just like her actions had been dictated by her own issues.

None of which mattered when she hurt so badly she wondered if she'd ever recover. Her heart was well and truly broken for the first time. She couldn't do anything about that, but she could work on her problems and fix her life as best she could.

Heading for her purse, she pulled out the social worker's card, hoping to make an appointment for early next week.

She needed help for herself.

And if she happened to convince Ian she not only loved him but was trying to get beyond her fears, well, her future was definitely bright. If he was finished with her regardless? She brushed at her wet cheeks. Well, she'd just have that much more to discuss in therapy.

* * *

Sending Riley's things back to her had nearly destroyed him. Still, he'd done what he had to do, ridding himself of all reminders, going back to the solitary way he'd lived before. Her scented items no longer sat in his bathroom surrounding his razor and toothbrush. Her clothes no longer hung in his closet. He now had an empty drawer where her sexy underwear used to be. No, she hadn't been with him long, but she'd made her mark.

He'd made room. Let her into his life.

And he missed her.

It'd been two weeks since the episode with her father, and staying away from her at work was giving him an ulcer. He was a nasty bastard with his sisters, his brothers steered clear, and his mother liked to berate him often about letting Riley slip through his fingers. Olivia had a big mouth.

"Shit." He never used to brood about women.

He had a breakfast date with his mother this morning, and if he could keep their conversation off Riley, he just might survive this day.

He strode into the restaurant his mother had chosen, but instead of finding her waiting at a table, he found his father.

"Oh hell no." Ian spun around, turning to go.

"Ian. Don't walk out on me."

He clenched his fists as he pivoted back and strode to the table where his father now stood. "But you had no trouble doing the same to me. To *us*."

"That's right. I did it. Now sit down and listen to my side for once."

Ian reared back, both at the admission of guilt and the fact that his father demanded to be heard. He hesitated a brief moment.

"I suggest you sit and talk to me. Unless you want to spend the rest of your life not only resenting me but giving up on the woman you love."

"My mother sent you here."

"Yes."

"To set me straight."

"Right again."

In other words, if he didn't have this talk, his mother would make sure she sat him down and did it herself. But for some reason, she'd decided to ask *him* to do it instead.

"Let's get this over with." Ian pulled out a chair and sat down.

His father did the same.

"I have no excuse for what I did. Your mother and I had an arrangement. I not only violated the sanctity of marriage by cheating, but I was a shitty father."

"To some of us," Ian muttered.

Robert braced his arms on the table. "To all of you. Savannah knew about your mother. I'm not sure which of the kids knew too, but trust me when I say, they didn't like me not being married to their mother, and when I told them about all of you—they resented being the illegitimate ones."

His words gave Ian pause. Not once had he thought about Alex and his siblings getting short shrift. Not. Once.

He pinched the bridge of his nose. "What's your point?"

"You are not making this easy." Robert shook his head, but Ian had to give the man credit, he didn't get up and leave. No, he stuck it out.

"Did you really expect me to?"

"My point is, none of you have good reason to trust or believe in people. The thing is, you underestimate people. You underestimate yourself. Look at what you've done for your sisters. For your mother. You've been their rock."

Compliments? From Robert Dare?

"Look at what you're capable of, and now let me ask you, are you really going to give up on Riley when she needs you the most?"

"Now we get to the point. You really think I'm going to sit and listen to you give me advice on love?"

His father grinned. "At least I know you love her. There's a place to start."

Ian sat back in his chair and groaned. "Yes. I love her. But she—"

"No buts, boy. If your mother hadn't said yes to marrying me, things would have been different. If she hadn't said, 'I might love someone else, but my father's sick so I have to marry a man of my parents' choosing'…well, I wouldn't have you wonderful children I don't deserve. But she'd have the man she really loved."

Ian's eyes opened wide at his father's full knowledge of his mother's emotions and feelings.

"Don't look so shocked. I knew I wasn't it for her. To say we didn't have a shot? Well, that's an understatement. But you and Riley? What could possibly be holding you back except for the fact that my behavior left you unable to trust or hold on to a good woman?"

Ian grew dizzy.

A waitress started toward them from across the room, and Robert shook his head. She stepped back.

"What do you know about Riley?" Ian asked, suddenly hungry for information about her. Starved, in fact.

"I only know what your brother told me."

Ian held back the word *half.*

"Which is?"

"The concussion's getting better, and she's moved back home."

"Into her piece-of-shit apartment?" His voice rose, and the older couple sitting next to him frowned at him, but Ian didn't care.

Robert shook his head. "Your brother and I agree about her living arrangements."

"She got a raise. She can afford a much safer place to live."

"Therapy costs a lot of money," his father said. "I didn't say that out loud, did I?"

Suddenly needing a caffeine boost, Ian gestured to the waitress, who bounced over with a smile. "What can I get for you?"

"Coffee, black, please."

She glanced at Robert. "Refill on the decaf. Thanks."

"Decaf, huh?" Ian asked when the waitress had walked away. "I remember Mom always having your coffee ready in a travel mug whether you were leaving for work or for the airport. Strong, black, no sugar." The memory took him by surprise.

He'd suppressed so many of his early childhood memories, the good and the bad, not wanting any part of his past, because any time he remembered, he hurt. Suddenly the hurt wasn't as sharp.

It wasn't the years that had dulled the pain, it was the changes in him. The softening. He knew he had Riley to thank for that.

"Therapy, huh?" he asked his father.

"You didn't hear it from me. I just thought if you realized how much of an effort she was making to deal with her past, maybe you would do the same. I'd ask you to do it for yourself, but I have a hunch I'd have more success if it was for her."

Ian frowned. "Because you know me so well?" he asked with no heat to his words. Not anymore. Though he didn't think he'd ever forgive and forget, holding on to so much hatred had taken so much out of him.

His walls had walls.

And those walls had kept Riley out. Even when he thought he'd let her in, he'd been pushing her away. How the fuck else had he walked out on her in the hospital? Self-loathing filled him at the thought, and Ian rose from his seat.

"Going to get your girl?" his father asked.

"Don't think this was a bonding moment," Ian said.

"Wouldn't dream of it," his father said, raising his coffee cup in a mock toast.

Ian's lips turned upward despite himself.

*   *   *

Riley worked late, not minding since she didn't have anything to rush home for. She typed up the last report of the day and organized her desk for the morning. But now she was ready to shut her computer and head back to her lonely, empty apartment, when her instant message chime went off.

She glanced at the monitor, hoping Dylan hadn't found a reason for them to stay even later. She was exhausted. She hadn't been getting much sleep since the incident with her father. Since she'd left Ian's and had gone back to sleeping alone in her own bed.

She looked at the screen, and her heart nearly stopped beating in her chest.

Ian: I need to speak to you.

She blinked, certain she was misreading. He'd avoided her since her return to work. She hadn't bumped into him in the hall nor had he sought her out. He hadn't called to check on her either. He'd just cut ties, and damned if that didn't hurt. After the longest month of her life, he was asking for her now?

She knew he couldn't want anything job related. She didn't work under him.

Her pulse began to race as she typed back.

Riley: Just leaving for the day. Will stop by on my way out.

Ian: I'll be waiting.

Her nerves kicked in as she powered down her computer and grabbed her purse, shutting the light off as she walked out of her office.

After five, support staff was gone for the day, and she knocked on his door, letting herself in.

He rose as soon as she stepped inside. "Lock the door," he said by way of greeting.

She automatically did as he asked, closing them in his office. Alone. Beneath her collar, she began to perspire from sheer nerves because she knew, no matter why he'd called her in here, they'd be having it out.

Possibly for good.

As usual for this time of day, his jacket was off, hung on a hook on his door, his tie was undone, and the top buttons on his dress shirt open. He looked scruffy and hot, but as sexy as he appeared, he also looked tired, dark circles shadowing his eyes, and she wondered if he'd lost as much sleep as she had since they'd been apart.

"How are you?" he asked, his searing gaze raking her over.

"Fine. Apparently I have a hard head." She knocked on her skull with her knuckles.

He didn't laugh. "Don't joke about what that bastard did to you."

"Well, I'm not going to cry about it." She'd done enough of that over Ian and her father both. After a lifetime of abuse, she still shed a tear over the kind of parent she had and the way he treated her.

"You look good," Ian said, sounding relieved. "I was worried."

"Bullshit." The words were out before she could think, taking her by surprise.

He reared back, staring at her.

"What? You want me to think you actually care? Is that why you walked out on me at the hospital and I haven't heard from you since?"

From the minute she'd entered this office, she'd felt her emotions brewing below the surface. She wasn't surprised they were coming out now. She'd spent so much time first berating herself for violating Ian's trust and then missing the good times they'd shared, she hadn't allowed her anger at him to truly surface. But as she stood here now, it was alive and vibrating within her.

"Go on," he said in a deceptively calm voice.

She flexed her fingers and decided to take her therapist's advice. Of course, she'd only had two sessions, but they'd been plenty productive. The first lesson? Let yourself feel. The second? Express those feelings before they eat you alive.

What was the worst thing that could happen? Ian had already abandoned her. She strode up to his desk, bracing her arms on the wooden top.

"My father slapped me. My head slammed against a brick wall. And you didn't come in to see if I was okay."

His eyes darkened, and his cheeks burned with what she'd like to think was embarrassment.

"The doctor came out with an update on your condition," he said.

"Oh. That makes it all better," she said, her temper rising.

"I never said it did."

His placid demeanor drove her insane. "I know I screwed up by not coming to you about my father's threats, but I had my reasons. I wanted the chance to explain them to you, but you wouldn't give me the chance."

She straightened and walked to his side of the desk, stepping into his personal space. "You dumped me on Alex and took off, never to be heard from again. Did you feel better after?" She shoved at his chest, hurt and so very betrayed. "Hmm? Did punishing me for defying you make you happy, Ian?" She shoved at him again.

He grabbed her wrist. "Nothing about how I handled this makes me happy. I was an arrogant ass. Is that what you want to hear? I thought if I laid down the law that you'd have to come to me first. Always. Then I'd have—"

"Control," she said at the same time as him.

"Exactly," he muttered.

"Well, I hope your precious control keeps you warm at night," she snapped at him.

"It doesn't."

"Good." Because she was lonely too.

He lifted a strand of her hair and twisted it between his fingers. She felt the pull straight through to her skin. It was the start of him getting to her—if she allowed him to.

She hadn't decided yet. "I'm human, which means I'm going to make my own decisions. And I'm going make mistakes," she told him.

A smirk edged the corners of his mouth.

"Unbelievable. You're laughing?"

He shook his head. "No, I'm just realizing you're smarter than I've ever been."

She tipped her head to one side. "Say that again?"

"Hell no. It's taken me too long to catch up," he muttered, more to himself than to her.

"Meaning?" she asked, her tone weary even to her.

He cupped her chin in his hand, just begging her to turn into him and find comfort. And she was tired. So tired of riddles and talking in circles. Tired of being alone.

His thumb caressed her jaw, and she couldn't help but stare into his eyes.

"Meaning, I love you," he said in a strong voice.

Riley gasped. "You—"

"I love you." His eyes were warm.

No longer that steely grey. She couldn't name the color, just the temperature in their depths. And there was heat. Lots and lots of heat. Everything inside her melted, at both his expression and the words she'd longed to hear.

"You're strong enough to overcome your past, and you're strong enough to deal with me. From the minute you walked into that ballroom, you were it for me," he said in a gruff, emotional tone she'd never heard from him before.

She swallowed past the lump in her throat. "How do I know you won't find some reason to push me away again?"

His hand remained on her cheek. "You trust me. How do I know you won't leave me for a better bet?"

"You trust *me*," she said, a slow grin spreading across her face.

Then she did the one thing that guaranteed him she understood. She grasped his wrist and turned her head, easing her cheek into his palm, accepting him and opening herself to *them*.

"I love you too, Ian."

The words reverberated in his brain until finally settling in his heart. She meant it. More important, *he believed it.*

He lifted her up and seated her on the desk, stepping between her legs. "I'm not sure how I got so lucky, but I won't be screwing this up."

She wound her arms around his neck. "How about you just screw me instead? How's that for a play on words?"

"Not funny." He leaned in, touching his nose to hers. "I'll be making love to you, not screwing you. And that's something you'd better remember."

He eased her skirt up around her legs, pulling off her barely there panties. "I think you should give up on underwear too," he informed her. "It'll make my life so much easier."

"Works for me," she said as her trembling fingers fumbled with his belt buckle, finally opening his pants.

He stepped back long enough to drop his trousers and kick them aside. He came back to her, taking his time, allowing his cock to slide up and down her sex. He couldn't refrain from glancing down, viewing his glide against her slick folds.

She answered with a soft moan. "I didn't think we'd be like this again," she whispered.

Knowing he'd broken her heart, he swore to himself he'd do everything possible to mend it and keep her whole for the rest of her life.

His gaze never leaving hers, he eased himself inside her slowly, reveling in the feel of her internal muscles as she clasped and clutched around his shaft.

She braced herself on her elbows, locking her legs around his waist, holding him in place.

"I love you," he said, thrusting deep.

Her eyes opened wide, and she moaned at the intimate contact.

"I love you too," she said. "So much."

With her words came soul-shattering emotion, as he made her his, settling so far inside her she became part of him. And every time he breathed, the base of his cock rubbed her clit, bringing them both closer to completion.

One good drive into her again and he'd come, but he didn't want to take her hard and fast and lose the beauty of the moment. Instead, he rocked against her, over and over, rolling his hips against hers, letting her soft breaths, clutching fingers, and wet heat work their own brand of magic.

He leaned in and pressed his lips against hers just as she started to come. She tugged at his hair with her fingers and rolled her hips, bucking against him. His cock grew rigid, his entire body tripping in ecstasy, feeling every second of her release.

"Oh, Ian! Love you, love you, love you!"

Her continuing chant triggered his release, and he began to thrust, his body consumed by the biggest tidal wave of heat and sensation he'd ever experienced. He was overwhelmed by the feelings and emotion pulsing through him as he spilled himself inside her. To his shock, she continued to pulse around him, aftershocks or a continuation of her equally explosive climax.

Unwilling to separate, he remained inside her and stroked her hair as they both came down.

"Ian?"

"Hmm?"

"Next time, you can tie me up," she murmured.

And damned if his cock didn't twitch in agreement. He appreciated that she might want to give him what she thought he needed, but the truth was, all he needed was Riley. The rest didn't matter.

He reluctantly pulled out of her. He headed for the bathroom, returning with a wet cloth. After taking care of her, he lifted her into his arms and moved them to the couch, where she cuddled on top of him, her head resting on his shoulder.

They lay in silence for a while, her rhythmic breathing reassuring him she wasn't going anywhere ever again.

"I'm seeing a therapist," she said softly.

Her sudden revelation surprised him, but he was glad she decided to confide in him. "Is it helping?"

"It is." She paused. "I need to tell you what happened with my father."

He nodded, needing to hear it too. "I assume he called and asked for money."

"Mmm-hmm. He saw the photos of us and decided you were his ticket to a windfall. He threatened to create a scandal that would embarrass you and the team. He swore you would drop me like the trash I always was." She shuddered as she spoke, and he realized the awful lies she'd grown up hearing about herself.

He tightened his arms around her and tried like hell to suppress the anger reverberating through him. She didn't need that from him now.

"I knew you wouldn't care, but I did. I didn't want to bring that kind of humiliation into your life, or your family's. None of you needed or deserved that."

"How about next time, you let me decide what I need?"

She nodded into his chest. "The thing is, even though he didn't hit me when I was younger, he made sure I knew my place. That I wasn't worth a damned thing, and those feelings came flooding back. I just wanted to fix it myself and make him go away. But when I got to the pawnshop, I couldn't do it."

Ian stilled. "But your father had the necklace in his hand. I just assumed you were giving it to him to sell."

She lifted herself up and straddled his waist. "No. I was going to pawn the necklace and give him the money at some point in the future. But I changed my mind. I couldn't do it. I couldn't give in to him one more time in my life, and I really couldn't part with the necklace you'd given me."

She reached up, her expression crestfallen when she realized the pendant was no longer there.

He could fix that, but he wanted her to finish unburdening herself first.

"I stood in the pawnshop and decided right then to go to you, so we could figure out what to do together. But when I walked out, my father was there, demanding the cash, and you know the rest."

Yeah. He knew. "Riley, you have to know you're worth everything to me. You make me a better man. And I'm so damned sorry I wasn't there when you needed me afterwards."

Her eyes filled, and his heart squeezed tightly. He hated causing her any kind of pain.

"You're here now."

"And I'm not going anywhere ever." He'd been without her, and he wasn't going back to that empty place again.

"Which reminds me. The reason I called you in here in the first place. Scoot over."

She slid off him, and he headed to his desk, coming back with two boxes. He handed her the long one first.

She opened it and squealed with delight. "My necklace!"

"I called the police and managed to convince them to return it to me after your father pleaded guilty."

"The district attorney called me to approve the deal."

"You're okay with the five years?"

She nodded. "As long as he's behind bars and I get a restraining order when he gets out, I'm okay."

Ian wouldn't let the man anywhere near her, but it was a discussion for far in the future.

He was more interested in focusing on the present. He lifted the necklace, and she raised her hair so he could replace it on her neck, where it belonged.

"I had the clasp fixed, and they cleaned it too."

She turned and kissed him. "Thank you." She touched the pendant. "I feel like you're always with me when I wear it."

"Then I hope you'll feel the same way about its mate."

She narrowed her gaze, wrinkling her nose in curiosity as he handed her the small box. "Ian?" she asked, her voice trembling.

He understood because his insides were a quaking mess.

Her hands shook as she lifted the top off the box, revealing the match to the pendant in ring form. A pear-shaped diamond that was too big, he knew, but he didn't care.

Corny as it was, he dropped to one knee. "Marry me," he said as she stared open-mouthed at the ring.

"Was that a question or a demand?" she asked, half laughing, half crying.

He grinned. "Still working on that part of me."

She met his gaze, her expression solemn. "I don't want to change you completely. I just need—"

He grasped her wrist. "I know what you need, and I want to be the one to give it to you."

"Tell me that includes you keeping control in the bedroom, because there are places I really don't mind you taking over."

"Is that a yes to my proposal?" he asked, his heart still hammering hard in his chest.

She wriggled her fingers in front of him. "Yes. Yes!"

He slid the ring onto her finger, grateful his sister had guessed her finger size correctly.

He rose and settled back on the couch, pulling her into his arms.

She sighed and snuggled close.

He didn't know how long they lay, her heart beating against his chest, but it was long enough for everything inside him to settle and for him to find the peace that had always eluded him.

Peace he sensed he'd now have, every day for the rest of his life, because he'd finally done what he'd always thought was impossible. He'd dared to love. And he had Riley to thank for teaching him how.

EPILOGUE

6 Months Later

Surrounded by his siblings, real and half, Alex nursed a beer as he glanced around his half brother's apartment. Everyone seemed to be having a good time. The food was phenomenal, Ian having spared no expense. He was doing his damnedest not to follow up every thought of Ian with an expletive or complaint, but old habits were hard to break.

The lovebirds couldn't take their hands off each other. Considering this was an engagement party, as well as a redo of the family event he'd botched a few months ago, Alex figured that was to be expected.

He wondered how long he had to stay before he could bow out and not have it look suspicious.

"What's with the scowl?" his sister Sienna asked.

"I'm not scowling." Was he?

"You're okay, right?" She wrapped her arms around him for a tight hug.

"Of course I am. Why wouldn't I be?"

She frowned at him. "You can fool the others, but I know you. You're jealous of Ian and Riley, and I'm worried about you."

Her words hit him where it hurt. "I am not jealous."

She settled her hands on her hips. "You've had Riley to yourself for years. Then Ian comes along and...well, you wouldn't be human if you weren't a little envious of what they have."

Even if he was, Alex wouldn't admit it out loud. Not even to the sister he loved. "It's fine. I want her to be happy, even if it is with him." He nodded toward Ian, doing his best to keep his expression neutral.

"Are you sure you aren't...a little bit in love with her?" Sienna asked.

Alex blanched. "Hell no. That'd be the same as thinking of you that way."

Sienna raised one eyebrow. "That was a quick denial."

"Look, maybe once, a long time ago..." He shook his head, not wanting to remember or even admit that, yeah, he'd once had feelings for Riley. Feelings that had been in no way brotherly.

Then he'd kissed her, she'd freaked out, saying they were such good friends, why ruin it, and he'd agreed. Quickly. Better that than to lose her, which seemed a certainty given that she clearly hadn't felt the same way about him.

Since then, he hadn't had to worry about her finding anyone serious, until Ian. His half brother. Well, whatever. The families were making their peace, and he had to live with it.

"Yeah, I thought so." Sienna clasped her small hand in his. "I just think facing your feelings is better than avoiding them. You don't have to tell anyone else, but I'm here for you, okay?"

He shook his head hard to clear his thoughts. "Hey, I said maybe, a long time ago. Not anymore. I'm fine." And he was, except…Ian and Riley's engagement made the stark contrast of his life clear.

He had his bimbos, and Riley? She had a soon-to-be husband and a life that didn't include him. Certainly not the way it used to.

"Okay. I'll accept that for now. I'm going to talk to Mom, okay?"

Another weird thing. Ian had invited their father and Savannah. Talk about making a huge concession and reaching out. Even Alex had to admire the man for that.

"Hi!" Riley walked over, a glass of champagne in hand. "I know you're not having the best time, but I'm really glad you're here."

He shook his head. "I'm having a good time," he lied. "And I love you. I wouldn't be anywhere else. You're happy, so I'm happy." And that much he meant. Absolutely.

Female laughter captured his attention, and he turned toward the sound. Not far from where he and Riley stood, Ian spoke to a beautiful blonde. She wore a fitted black skirt that hugged delicious-looking curves and a purple satin top that covered more of her than it exposed. He was used to women who flaunted their assets and would definitely consider himself a breast man. He couldn't see a damned thing about this woman's cleavage, and yet he couldn't tear his gaze away. Something about the way she held herself, so tightly composed and not overtly sexual, appealed to him on a visceral level.

Really unlike his usual type too. Huh.

"Who is she?" he asked Riley, thinking that something about her looked familiar.

"You don't recognize her, do you?" Riley laughed. "That's Madison Evans, the social worker you met at the hospital after..." Her voice trailed off, and he understood her not wanting to mention or think about her father, who Alex hoped was miserable during his stint behind bars.

"No shit?" He blinked. This woman with the flowing, blonde hair was the same female who'd all but ignored him the one and only time they'd met.

He shouldn't be shocked though. She'd worn a prim little skirt then, paired with a blouse that hid her assets, and even then, he'd been drawn to her. It'd pissed him off too. Not because she hadn't recognized him, as unusual as that was in his world. But because she hadn't given him a second glance. Madison Evans had bruised his ego as much as she'd surprised him by attracting his attention in the first place.

"I know that you saw her for a couple of sessions afterwards, but if she's your therapist, what's she doing here?"

"I finished therapy." Riley smiled. "I really didn't want to spend years rehashing things. Anyway, Madison and I became friendly, and I don't have many close women friends." Riley shrugged, as if that explained it all.

He supposed it did.

"Why are you so interested in her?" Riley asked. "Because I noticed the same reaction the first time you laid eyes on her."

Alex cocked an eyebrow. He'd been wondering that himself. Something about the woman called to him in ways he didn't understand. He shrugged, deciding he didn't need to understand, he needed to get her attention.

"Uh oh. What's that sudden focus in your eyes?" Riley waved her hand in front of his face. "You look… determined."

He'd been bored at this party, looking for something—or someone—to capture his interest. He'd found her.

He started toward her when Riley's voice stopped him. "She's not your usual fare." Her tone held a wealth of warning.

Alex turned and grinned. "That's what I'm counting on."

Dare to Desire – Alex & Madison

Coming Spring 2014

Thank you so much for reading Ian's story. The Dare to Love series will continue in 2014 with Alex's story – *Dare to Desire*. Stay up to date with what's happening with the Dare to Desire series by visiting these links:

Sign up for my newsletter:
www.carlyphillips.com/newsletter-sign-up/

My website:
www.carlyphillips.com

Follow me on Twitter:
www.twitter.com/carlyphillips

Friend me on Facebook:
www.facebook.com/carlyphillipsfanpage

Follow or Friend me on Goodreads:
http://www.goodreads.com/author/show/10000.Carly_Phillips/

Please read on for a sneak peek of PERFECT TOGETHER, the last book in Carly's Serendipity series, Berkley, out February 4, 2014.

One

There was something about being a Marsden that made people think if they asked him for a favor, Sam, the younger brother, and the *good* cop, would be nice and accommodating. Take how his sister-in-law, Cara, was looking at him with big, pleading eyes, fully expecting him to agree to her beyond-unreasonable request.

"There is no way in hell I'm going on a date with Margie Simpson." Sam Marsden glared at Cara, a woman he usually also called his best friend, from across their respective desks at the Serendipity police station.

"Her last name is Stinson, not Simpson, and you know it." Cara frowned back at him. "Come on, Sam. Her parents are the biggest donors for the Women's Heart Health fund-raiser, and the Serendipity Police Department is a co-sponsor. Do you want to be the one to tell the hospital, who will be the recipient of that shiny new medical equipment, that the Stinsons pulled their donation because one of our finest wouldn't escort their daughter?"

"She's more like a pit bull," Sam muttered. "And isn't there another single cop you can get to take her? What about Hendler?"

"He's too old."

"Martini?"

She shook her head. "Too young. Besides, Margie wants to go with you."

He shuddered. "All the more reason for me to say no. I don't want to give her the wrong idea." Margie was one of those women who assumed that just a look imparted male interest. Sam didn't want to go there. No way, nohow.

"Are you giving my wife a hard time?" Sam's brother, Mike, strode over to Cara's desk and placed a possessive hand on her shoulder.

"More like she's giving me one. Call her off, will you?" Sam asked.

Mike laughed and shook his head. "I like my life just the way it is. Sorry, bro. You're on your own."

Sam rolled his eyes. Ever since his bachelor brother had fallen—hard—for Sam's sometime partner, Cara, he was now wrapped around his wife's cute little cowboy boots—when she wasn't in uniform, that is. Where she went, Mike followed. Sam was happy for him. Problem was, Sam's single friends were dwindling fast. First Dare Barron, then Mike, and even their sister, Erin, had fallen.

Sam wasn't jealous, but he could admit that his life and the routines he'd always enjoyed were growing stale around him. But that didn't mean he was open to marriage, let alone escorting the female from hell, even for a good cause.

Cara rolled a pencil between her palms. "Do you already have a date?" she asked.

"Hell, no," Mike said, before Sam could answer. "He hasn't dated anyone in longer than I can remember. In fact, the last woman who remotely interested him—"

No, he would not let his brother go *there*. "Don't you have an office to get back to?" Sam pointed to the police chief's workroom at the back of the stationhouse.

Mike grinned. "Not when this is so much more fun."

Cara elbowed him in the stomach. "Go. I'll have more luck if you aren't here poking fun at him and making this worse."

Mike shrugged. "Hey, it's not my fault he's such an easy target."

"Now that you're happily married, you're an even bigger pain in the ass," Sam muttered.

Mike smirked and kissed his wife on the lips, lingering way too long before he finally walked—make that swaggered—away.

"Get a room."

"You too could find true love," Cara said, leaning closer. "We all want that for you."

But Sam didn't want that for himself. He'd tried, come close, and failed in the biggest possible way. As a cop, he trusted his instincts, but when it came to women? To relationships? To personal choices? Not so much.

His so-called gut instinct had hurt one good friend, and his gullibility had led to him being betrayed by his fiancée and best friend. His family knew only some of the reasons he remained wary of trusting his personal instincts, and with his siblings settled down, Erin with a husband and a baby, they'd all turned up the pressure on him.

Cara leveled him with a serious stare. "I'm not asking you to marry Margie, just accompany her to the benefit. Make nice and go home. Can you do that for me? For Mike and the police station? Please?" Cara batted her eyelashes over her big blue eyes.

She'd been his best friend long before she became involved with Mike, and he'd have thought he was immune—except now she was also his family and he didn't like turning her down. Besides, as she'd pointed out, the fund-raiser was for a good cause and he'd be representing the police force.

He blew out a disgusted breath. "You're only doing this because I can't say no to you," Sam muttered, shuddering at the thought of accompanying the one woman in town who sent fear into any single man's heart.

"Is that a yes?" Cara tapped her pencil against the blotter on the desk, her expression almost gleeful.

"Yeah," he muttered, knowing he would absolutely live to regret the decision.

"Yay!" She jumped up and hugged him tight before resettling herself into the chair behind her desk. "This is *perfect*! One huge problem taken care of. I knew I could count on you."

Yeah, perfect, Sam thought, hating that word even more than usual.

"Hey, I promise Mike and I will stick by you all night. I won't leave you alone with that leech."

Sam narrowed his gaze. "So now you admit she's a leech."

Cara didn't look up or meet his gaze, but the red flush in her cheeks gave her away. Yeah, he was a patsy for his sister-in-law and a good cause.

"You know," Cara said, peering out from beneath her long fringe of lashes, "you could avoid this whole kind of thing if you'd just—"

Find a woman of his own. "Let it go," he said in response to her unspoken words.

"Okay, but Mike's right. The last woman who interested you was—"

"Let. It. Go." Sam set his jaw.

"Fine. I won't say her name." Cara buried herself in work at her desk, but she'd accomplished her mission.

She'd brought up the one female in more than a decade who'd made Sam want to drop his guard and rethink his vow not to get emotionally involved with any woman ever again. But Nicole Farnsworth, the raven-haired beauty who'd triggered his current state of discontent, had left town months ago and she wasn't coming back.

*   *   *

Nicole Farnsworth packed up her clothing and the last of her things, trying to convince herself she was moving, not running away. In fact, she'd planned to leave Manhattan since deciding to end her engagement, but now instead of just the excitement of beginning a new life, she felt the dual need to flee. She closed her eyes and drew a deep breath. Nothing she could do but go—get away—and do some soul-searching, during which she hoped to find clarity. But what clarity was there when she knew she held people's livelihoods and even freedom in her hands?

The doorbell rang and she looked into the peephole, unwilling to take chances by just opening her door. She stared into the familiar if unwelcome face of her mother, as usual, perfectly dressed in her Chanel jacket and wool slacks.

Suppressing a groan, she opened the door and let Marian Farnsworth inside.

Before Nicole could say hello, her mother launched into one of her typical tirades. "No sane woman breaks off her engagement to a handsome, extremely wealthy man. One you grew up with, might I remind you? He and his family are in business with your father. What were you thinking?"

Nicole walked into the family room and leaned against the nearest wall, knowing not to give her mother an edge by sitting down "I was thinking that I shouldn't marry a man I don't love."

Her mother joined her in the room filled with the remaining boxes waiting to be loaded into her car. She folded her arms across her chest and pinned Nicole with her disappointed stare. "What does love have to do with anything?"

Nicole did not want an explanation for that bit of insanity. It meant she'd have to look more deeply than she cared to into her parents' marriage. Instead she drew a deep breath and promised herself she'd be on her way soon.

"Nicole, it's insane to think someone like you needs to worry about a love match."

She shrugged. "You know as well as I do, sanity doesn't run in our family."

"Don't talk that way about your sister," her mother chided, always looking to hide Victoria's mental instability, as if being bipolar carried a stigma Marian couldn't bear to admit to in her family.

The irony was Nicole hadn't been talking about Victoria, merely making a not-so-subtle joke.

"Darling, you need to call Tyler and beg him to forgive you."

This, Nicole had heard before. "No." And she had more important things to worry about than her mother's reaction to her breaking her engagement. Like the illegal activities Nicole had overheard her ex-fiancé's father and his accountant discussing—and what she was going to do about them. Considering, as her mother reminded her, that the partnership of Farnsworth and Stanton Financial Investments affected both families, Nicole needed distance to study all the angles.

Such as, did Nicole's father know that his partner was accepting money from mob-connected companies and funneling that money into investments from which they all made millions? Did her ex-fiancé Tyler know?

"Nicole," her mother said, snapping her fingers in front of her face. "You're not listening to me."

"Because I have things on my mind. Like moving." Not just so she could get away and think, but so she could forge a new life where people would get to know and like Nicole for herself, not her family's connections.

Her mother's face flushed red at the reminder. It was amazing how the woman could ignore the evidence in front of her: the boxes, packing tape, and clothing covered by heavy-duty bags. "You have to reconsider. This whole situation is humiliating in the extreme. Not to mention, you have a job. Tyler's mother is running for borough president and you're her number one fund-raiser. She needs you."

"I gave her notice. My assistant is capable and ready to take over. She'll be fine."

"You'll cause a rift between the families," her mother pushed on.

Nicole stiffened, not missing the irony. Growing up, she'd sought her parents' approval and attention by being good and kind and perfect—without success. But now, when she no longer cared what her family thought of her choices, she'd accomplished her goal. Her mother was here, paying attention to her life, begging her to help them.

"The Stantons won't hold my choices against you."

"Nicole!"

"No. Stop it. I told you before. I am not going back to Tyler. I don't love him. I should have realized it long before now." And the reasons why she hadn't were glaringly obvious in light of her mother's callous disregard of her daughter's feelings.

She'd desperately wanted someone to love and approve of her, and Tyler, unlike her parents, had been kind and caring. He paid attention to her and he'd given her everything she'd yearned for in her emotionally deprived life. Unfortunately, Nicole had mistaken her gratitude toward him for love, and she'd hurt Tyler in the process.

It had taken her sister's downward spiral and Nicole's resulting meeting with a sexy small-town cop to point out to her exactly what she didn't feel for her then-fiancé. Desire, excitement, the pounding of her heart every time he was near. She'd settled for less every minute of her childhood. She couldn't bring herself to do it in marriage.

Nicole realized her mother was still staring at her with frustration and disappointment in her expression.

"It's better I made the decision now than after the wedding," Nicole told her.

Marian huffed. "Just when did I teach you that fairy tales come true?" she asked in disgust.

Nicole met her mother's gaze. "You never did."

Without so much as a word, not *good luck* or even *good-bye*, her mother turned and stormed out the door.

Nicole swallowed the lump in her throat. Her mother hadn't changed in all of Nicole's twenty-eight years. But Nicole had. With this move, she wasn't looking for some improbable happy ending. All she wanted—no, craved—was a life of her own that fulfilled her dreams and desires, and not those of her impossible-to-please family.

So she was heading to the one place where she'd found a sense of peace despite the insanity—no pun intended—that had brought her to the sleepy upstate town. She hoped that once there, she'd figure out the right thing to do about the information she'd stumbled over.

Nicole was ready for Serendipity. She just hoped the people in Serendipity were ready for her.

* * *

One of the things Nicole liked about Serendipity was its old-fashioned charm. Where else could you find a diner-slash-restaurant named The Family Restaurant? After spending the morning moving into her new apartment over Joe's Bar, she decided to eat dinner out and go food shopping tomorrow.

She sat at the counter, happy to just soak in the atmosphere, and had just finished a delicious plate of meat loaf and mashed potatoes when a dark-haired woman approached her from behind the counter.

"Wait. I know you," the woman said, her gaze narrowing.

Nicole met the other woman's concerned stare, well aware of the reason for the worry in her eyes. The one thing that had concerned Nicole about moving here was being mistaken for her twin. But the pull of the small town had been strong, and despite Victoria's actions, people here hadn't judged Nicole, at least not once she'd tried desperately to help them find her twin.

Nicole wanted to give them the same benefit of the doubt. "I don't believe we've met."

"I'm Macy Donovan. Occasional hostess, waitress, you name it. My family owns the restaurant. Aren't you—"

"Nicole Farnsworth," she chimed in quickly.

"So you're not Victoria? The psychopath who—"

"No," Nicole said, cutting her off before she could elaborate on Victoria's crimes. When her sister went off her medication, anything could happen—and had. "She's my twin."

Macy's cheeks turned red in embarrassment. "Sorry, but she hurt a friend of mine and... Never mind."

Nicole winced. "I expected to deal with the fallout if I moved here."

Macy raised her eyebrows. "And yet you decided to settle in Serendipity?"

"Yes, I did." She squared her shoulders, intending to communicate to Macy Donovan that not only was she sure of her decision but she wasn't about to be bullied because of her sister's illness. Her twin was in a criminal mental health facility, living with the consequences of her actions.

"Listen, I'm blunt but I'm not judging you," the woman said. "Erin Marsden's my best friend, and your sister stalked her for months."

Nicole grimaced at the reminder.

"But Erin told me you helped them find where your sister was hiding out, and she said you came to town in the first place to warn her and Cole. So... truce?" Macy held out her hand.

Letting out a deep breath, Nicole accepted the other woman's peace offering. "Thanks." From inside her purse, her cell phone chimed, calling for her attention.

"I'm going to do a few things in the back. I'll come out again in a few minutes," Macy said, leaving her alone to take the call.

A quick look told her it was her ex-fiancé, so she blew out a breath and hit Decline. She'd explained everything in person and there was no reason to rehash things over the phone. His call only reminded her of what she still needed to deal with, but she wasn't any closer to a decision. Should she confront her father and ask what he knew of his partner's accounts? Should she ask Tyler?

She'd stood outside the office of her own father—a man she didn't know all that well, as he certainly never made an effort to spend time with her as a child—and as she raised her hand to knock on the open door, she'd *heard*. There'd been no question that she'd mistaken the spoken words.

Robert Stanton and the firm accountant had specifically said they were laundering money from the Romanovs, a father and son who were known art dealers in Los Angeles. The Russian mob, she thought, her stomach churning. Their entire business could crumble, not to mention they could all end up in prison. Her stomach in knots, she'd turned to run, but Nicole's father strode up to her at that very moment. He'd called out her name, which in turn brought Robert and Andre, the accountant, out into the hall to greet them.

The look Andre had given her chilled her even now. She told herself he couldn't possibly know she'd heard anything. But she had. Which meant she didn't need to worry just about her family and the business, but also about the men on the other side. Dangerous men.

Should she go to her father with the truth? If he already knew about his partner's illegal dealings, she wouldn't accomplish anything except to out herself. If Paul Farnsworth was in the dark, he probably wouldn't believe his daughter's word over his longtime partner's. Nicole's own mother would remain in useless denial even if confronted, and Tyler's mother's main source of campaign funds was her husband. No way would she risk using dirty money. So she ruled out her being aware. Which left the police—and she wasn't ready for that yet.

And what about Tyler? She knew he was honest to a fault. She couldn't imagine him allowing illegal dealings to go on, any more than she could envision his father involving him. He'd grown up as heir to the proverbial throne—entitled, privileged—and to his credit he rarely acted the role they'd bestowed on him. She had to assume they'd keep him squeaky clean.

But again, she couldn't rely on assumption. The unknown players were just too dangerous.

"So did you decide what you want?" Macy asked.

"Not yet." Nicole hadn't even looked at the menu.

Macy picked up a towel and wiped down the counter. "So what brings you to Serendipity?"

Easy answer, Nicole thought. "A fresh start."

Macy grinned. "Because you liked it so much your first time around?"

Nicole laughed, grateful for this chatty woman and the distraction she provided. "That too. Seriously. Considering the reason I was here, the place and the people made an impact."

Macy leaned on the counter. "It just so happens that there's a fund-raiser this weekend to raise money for women's heart health. I'm selling tickets and you should come!"

Nicole hesitated; the thought of walking into a big event all alone was not something she was ready to face. "I don't know. I mean, I'm new in town—"

"All the more reason to go where you can meet people! Dates aren't required. I'm not going with anyone, so we can hang out. What do you say?"

Nicole figured Macy was right, as far as it being a good way to get to know people, and now that Macy had invited her to join her, she felt more comfortable.

Before Nicole could answer, her new friend chimed in once more. "It's for a good cause. The police department is co-sponsoring the event, and since this place is basically like a doughnut shop for Serendipity's Finest, I agreed to pimp tickets for them. Please?" Macy was nothing if not persistent, and her enthusiasm was infectious.

So was the fact that the police sponsorship guaranteed Sam Marsden would be at the event. And she'd like to see him again... "Okay."

"Yay!" Macy's smile dimmed. "But it's expensive since it's a fund-raiser."

"How much?"

"Seventy-five dollars."

Nicole nodded. She had a plan for her life that included opening her own bake shop, but not right away. She needed to research the area, see if it could sustain what she had in mind. Which meant she needed a job while she plotted her future. In the meantime, she had the trust fund her grandparents had left her, something that irked her parents to no end, since it meant they couldn't control what she or Victoria did.

Nicole didn't plan to blow through the money frivolously, and she'd need it for her business venture, but it did enable her to rent the apartment and cover the cost of living until she got on her feet. As far as she was concerned, getting to know people in her new town and supporting a worthwhile cause certainly fell under that heading.

"No problem." She met Macy's gaze, and the other woman smiled wide.

"Great! Oh. Another thing."

Nicole leaned forward on her arms and waited. Clearly she'd met someone in the know.

"Cocktail attire."

"Also not a problem." Though she'd packed up everything she owned, thanks to Tyler and his mother's world that included formal and cocktail dresses, and she'd kept a few favorites.

"That was easy," Macy said.

Nicole grinned. "I try."

"So are you interested in a primer on your new hometown?"

"I'm all ears."

Macy propped a hip on the counter, relaxed and happy to chat. "Wednesday night is Ladies' Night at Joe's. You should join us—the *us* depends on who is free because there's been way too many marriages and babies lately, so the ladies and the men are dwindling. But not for you because you're new to all the men and they'll all be new to you. So you'll come to that too?"

Nicole nodded, pleased to have plans. "Absolutely."

"Great." Macy looked toward the front door and the family who'd entered. "I have to go seat people. If I don't have time to talk more today, I'll see you Wednesday? Seven p.m."

Nicole smiled as the other woman headed off to do her job.

She liked Macy Donovan, and it seemed like Macy had already accepted Nicole. She hoped everyone else in Serendipity felt the same way.

*   *   *

As on a typical Wednesday night, Sam met up with some guys from the station at Joe's Bar. Josh Mercer had bought the current round and the jokes were flowing freely. Mike and Cara walked in, followed by his sister, Erin, and her husband, Cole.

"Looks like it's family night," Sam said, calling them over. "How did you two get away?"

Erin had had a baby six months ago and rarely left her daughter's side.

His sister greeted him with a kiss on the cheek. "Mom showed up and practically shoved us out the door. She said we needed a break and she needed time with Angel." The hazel eyes she shared with Sam lit up when she mentioned her baby daughter.

Cole slipped an arm around Erin's waist, greeting Sam with a nod. "She's already called home twice to remind your mother about the time of her next bottle and what to do if she cries."

"Like she didn't raise three of us?" Sam teased his sister.

"Funny," Erin said to her brother. "And *he*"—she poked her husband with her elbow—"already called Mom to make sure she had our cell phones on speed dial."

Sam still couldn't believe they'd gone from his sister getting pregnant after a one-night stand with Cole Sanders, undercover cop with no intention of remaining in town, to being a happily married couple and overly concerned parents.

"All my favorite people are here!" Sam turned at the sound of Macy's voice.

Erin spun and gave her best friend a hug.

"How is that adorable goddaughter of mine?" Macy asked.

"Cute as ever." Erin beamed.

"Hon, want to go get a drink?" Cole asked her.

Erin nodded.

"Anyone else want anything?" Cole asked.

"I'm good," Macy said.

"Me too," Sam added.

Erin and Cole walked toward the bar, leaving Sam alone with Macy. She was his sister's best friend, so he was used to her being around.

"Hi, Macy. How are you?"

"Hi yourself." Her smile, as usual, was infectious. "I'm good. Busy as usual. You?"

He shrugged. "Same old."

She shook her head, her long dark hair falling over one shoulder, and sighed. "You so need to get laid."

Sam rolled his eyes, not surprised by her outgoing ways. In addition to her blunt manner, she was beautiful, sort of exotic, her Italian heritage showing through. If she hadn't been like family, he might have looked twice—until she started busting his balls, that is. She wasn't for him, but no doubt she'd give some guy a run for his money.

She glanced around, a frown furrowing her eyebrows. "Where's Nicole?"

Sam whipped his head around to meet her gaze. "Who?" He had to have heard wrong. That or it could be another Nicole. It was a common enough name.

Macy scanned the crowds before refocusing on Sam. "You probably know her? Nicole Farnsworth, the stalker's sister? She's new in town and renting the room over Joe's. I invited her to meet me here tonight." Macy glanced at her watch, and her concerned expression turned to a frown. "She's late. You haven't seen her, have you?"

Sam expelled a harsh breath. Nicole had moved here? Months of thinking about her and she was now as close as upstairs?

"Maybe she's uncomfortable, not knowing anyone... and considering I mistook her for her crazy sister at first .. I should go check on her." She shoved her glass at Sam. "Hold this for me?"

Sam shook his head. "I'll go."

Macy narrowed her gaze and stepped into Sam's direct path. "So you do know her."

He nodded, his heart racing at the thought of seeing her again. No woman had ever made him feel so many things in such a short time. Protective, aroused, attracted...

"And you're interested," Macy concluded in the wake of his silence.

"No comment. I'm going upstairs. You can hold down the fort here." This time he handed her his beer bottle.

Macy watched him, her stare too perceptive for his liking.

"And do not give my sister or brother the wrong impression. I just want to say hi and welcome her to town. Make sure she feels comfortable enough to come down and join us."

"If you say so, Detective," she said, using his brand-new moniker.

He still wasn't used to the title or the promotion, but he'd worked hard for it, and nepotism—his brother being chief—had nothing to do with his new position.

He turned and headed for the back entrance of the bar and slipped out the exit. As soon as he hit the top of the stairs and stood outside the apartment door, he paused. Everyone he knew had lived here at one time or another, from Faith and Kelly Barron, to his brother, Mike, and then Erin's husband, Cole. The place was a revolving door, a pit stop before people settled down for good.

Now Nicole.

He'd known her for a short time, when she'd been in Serendipity tracking her missing sister, who it turned out had been stalking Erin. Sam had arrested her lurking outside Erin's condo, assuming she was her psychotic twin. But there was nothing unstable about Nicole... and she'd made a profound impact on Sam. From her dark hair to her big beautiful blue eyes, he felt like he could see inside her soul.

On first meeting, she'd been scared, then defiant, but ultimately he came to admire how she'd handled herself while in that small interrogation room. But the real turning point between them had come when Cole barged in. She'd immediately turned to Sam, as if assuming she could trust him to look after her. She hadn't been wrong. And not just because he had a reputation for being the *good cop* in any scenario. With Nicole, the protective surge he'd experienced surpassed the normal doing of his job. It made no damned sense to him then, and it still didn't now. Hell, her draw scared him as much as it pulled him toward her.

Once her sister had been arrested, Nicole had gone back to the city where she belonged before Sam could act on any stupid sexual or deeper impulse he might have. He hadn't had an emotional connection with any female since Jenna's betrayal, and he wouldn't allow himself to be hurt that way again. But none of that seemed to matter now that *she* was back in town.

Sam couldn't imagine why Nicole had opted to move to Serendipity—but there was one way to find out. Raising his hand, he knocked on her door.

PERFECT TOGETHER by Carly Phillips
out February 4, 2014

Other Carly Phillips' Titles

Serendipity

(http://www.carlyphillips.com/category/books/?series=serendipity-series)

Serendipity

Destiny

Karma

Serendipity's Finest Series

(http://www.carlyphillips.com/category/books/?series=serendipitys-finest)

Perfect Fit

Perfect Fling

Perfect Together

Serendipity Novellas

(http://www.carlyphillips.com/category/books/?series=serendipity-novellas)

Kismet

Fated

Hot Summer Nights (Perfect Stranger)

Love Unexpected Series

(http://www.carlyphillips.com/category/books/?series=ebooks)

Perfect Partners

Solitary Man

The Right Choice

Midnight Angel

For a complete list of all my series and books, visit:
www.carlyphillips.com/category/books/

About the Author

N.Y. Times and *USA Today* Bestselling Author Carly Phillips has written over 40 sexy contemporary romance novels that today's readers identify with and enjoy. After a successful 15 year career with various New York publishing houses, Carly made the leap to Indie author, with the goal of giving her readers more books at a faster pace at a better price. She also hopes to rediscover the pure joy of writing without expectations. Carly lives in Purchase, NY with her family, two nearly adult daughters and two crazy dogs who star on her Facebook Fan Page and website. She's a writer, a knitter of sorts, a wife, and a mom. In addition, she's a Twitter and Internet junkie and is always around to interact with her readers.

Made in the USA
Lexington, KY
24 August 2014